Snapshots of China

Snapshots of
CHINA

Alison Mullins

Free Fall Publishing
119 S Fern Avenue
Wichita, KS 67213

www.alisonmullins.com

For Mom and Dad.

Your sacrifices for me and your willingness to not only let me walk this path, but also love and support me through it made the journey a joy.

"For everything there is a season, and a time for every matter under heaven: a time to weep, and a time to laugh; a time to mourn, and a time to dance."
Ecclesiastes 3:1, 4

CONTENTS

FOREWARD

When Alison and I first stepped off the plane in 2013, we had no idea what would lay in store for us on the other side of the world. And how could we? China was an entirely different country, with different food, a different language, different culture—well, different everything.

We had no idea about the adventures we would have and the stories we would tell. Adventures like riding camels through the Gobi Desert, searching out the ruins of the Great Wall in the dead of winter, riding e-bikes through typhoons, or wandering around a mountain in Hangzhou searching for a hotel because there was no room in the inn for foreigners.

We also had no idea about the souls we would meet. The students who couldn't speak a word of English, yet showed up to every class, clutching their notebooks and eventually becoming fluent through sheer determination. The students who saved us and paid our taxi fare after a pickpocketing. The students who came over for annual Christmas parties, drinking hot chocolate and decking the halls with us. The students who opened up about their beliefs, their fears, and their dreams over bowls of noodles at dinner.

We heard about their families. Celebrated their college graduations. Hugged them when they got accepted to foreign universities. Encouraged them after failed exams. Toasted them at their weddings.

All of these stories, all of these people, became a part of us.

There's no way to perfectly wrap up each person's story and each unique experience into a book. But isn't that true of everyone's life? The beauty of the human experience is that it cannot be replicated; it cannot be recounted in full; it cannot be repeated. All we can do is try to give others a glimpse into our experience.

The author Victor Hugo wrote, "Many great actions are committed in small struggles." This book is a collection of small struggles, an insight into a few moments of a person's life. Some are ordinary, some joyous, some anxious, some desperate, some iridescent.

From a lower-class worker dreaming about his daughter's future to a girl worried about never healing from a broken heart to a man who doesn't know where his home is anymore, all of these stories come together to create a mosaic of experiences.

How do you put into words the intricacies of a different culture, with all its different systems, ideologies, and traditions? The answer is: You don't. You can't. But maybe, as you see a snapshot of someone else's joys, their heartbreaks, and their struggles, you'll see all their wild complexities and recognize the similarities we all share—even across the globe.

Megan Hutchinson

INTRODUCTION

After a week in China, I was ready to write a book. After a year, I realized that I couldn't write anything because there's just too much to say. Now, after nearly nine years in China, I've realized I don't have to write about *everything* in order to share *something*. Because I love this country, I've decided to share small pieces of China in the form of short stories based on my own experiences or the experiences of friends and students I have met here. These stories are a mixture of a little fiction and a lot of truth. While some details have been added, they are largely based on true stories.

These stories are also Word Doodles (thank you to Miranda Regan for sharing this concept with me and quite possibly inventing the idea—I miss listening to you read your word doodles!). Word Doodles are short stories or character sketches written using two completely random words chosen by someone else. The challenge of a Word Doodle is to include those two randomly-chosen words in the story in some way. Sometimes an entire story is based on one of the words, and other times, they are simply sneaked into the story. I have included the randomly-chosen words at the beginning of each sketch. Each of my Word Doodles are also based in China about Chinese people or foreigners in China.

I wrote these stories just for fun. The random words helped to give me ideas and direction, and I wanted to practice writing more. But the more I wrote, the more I realized that these stories contain truths I want to share with you. I want more people to know about the daily life of strangers on the other side of the world. I want you to understand more about Chinese people and some of the cultural differences between Americans and Chinese. (While there are people from a variety of countries living in China, I focus mostly on Americans and their experiences as foreigners in another country simply because, as an American, that is what I am most familiar with.)

These stories may have started as a fun writing exercise, and I share that background with you because that is a part of what makes these stories special, but these stories are much more than a simple writing exercise. These stories contain truths I have learned as a teacher, friend, and girlfriend in China. It's been quite the experience, and I hope you enjoy reading about it as much as I've enjoyed living it and writing it.

Living the Dream

Ellie

Inspiration Words: LA and Terracotta

"Where is the international terminal?" Ellie asked someone with a nametag, hoping they could direct her to the right area.

"Go outside and turn left."

That sounds simple enough, Ellie thought as she thanked Jill with the nametag and dragged her suitcases toward the outside door. Once outside, the hot summer air sucked her breath away, but a few moments later, a breeze drifted through the concrete columns. Ellie studied her ticket before looking at the rows of numbered pillars. Gate B12, but everything around her still said A.

Why is no one else out here? Doesn't anyone else need to get to the international terminal? And why isn't my gate on any of the entrances? Ellie tried to stand tall as she dragged her two fifty-pound suitcases behind her. She wanted to look like she knew where she was going, even though she had no idea. A worker emptied the trash cans, ignoring Ellie as she stared in indecision. *Keep going or turn back?* This area looked like she was heading toward the parking garage, but she decided to try it anyway.

Several minutes later, she finally found the entrance to terminal and headed inside. She smiled as she noticed she was now surrounded by people. Apparently, everyone else had managed to find the international terminal as well. She followed the signs toward the departure area, checked her giant bags, and soon found herself sitting in a semi-uncomfortable chair at her gate. For the first time since arriving in LA, she took a deep breath and realized she was preparing for the final flight before her new life.

Xi'an (see-ahn). That's what the destination on her ticket said. *ee-ahn*. Ellie repeated the sounds slowly in her head, just as she remembered her grandma saying them. *Is that right? I hope I can say it properly, so people understand me.*

She reached into the pocket of her loose pants and grabbed the small form of a Terracotta Soldier. *What has this little man gotten me into?* she thought. She felt the rounded knot of hair at the top of his head and the lines on his body showing where his uniform was. While she stared at the screen above the airport desk, waiting for the "Now boarding" signal to show she should get in line, she thought about the first time she had held this little warrior in the palm of her hand.

"*China is a big place with a long history—5,000 years, as I've been told.*" Grandma smiled as she pressed a small soldier into the hand of each of her five grandkids. Ellie's four cousins had run off to start a war with the small soldiers, but Ellie wanted to hear more about China and her grandma's most recent trip to that country.

"*What was it like, Gramma?*"

"*Well, it's different now than it used to be. You know the first time I went was for an agricultural tour with your grandpa before you were born.*"

"*How is it different? And what's an agricultural tour?*"

"*An agricultural tour means people can go to another place to see how other people farm. I got to learn a lot about farming when I visited. Things have changed a lot since then, though-- well, for one thing, they found this little man and a lot of his friends. When I was there back in the 60s, they hadn't even found him yet. He was here, but hidden on a farm, buried like a secret under the ground.*"

"*Are Chinese people nice? Did you try Chinese food?*"

"*One question at a time now, little Ellie. Chinese people are just like other people; some of them are nice, and some of them are not as nice. As for the food, it was spiiiicy! Now go play with your cousins before your little soldier gets jealous!*"

Ellie did join in the games with her cousins, but she also kept thinking about that country so far away. She wondered if all Chinese people looked like the Terracotta Soldier she held in her small hand. She wondered if she would like Chinese spicy *food. She wondered about everything. She wondered if the kids there ever wanted to come here. But she couldn't imagine anyone wanting to leave a place as interesting as China to come to America. Ellie glanced at her cousins and brother as they played on the grass in the backyard. Playing war was not as interesting as hearing more of Grandma's stories.*

Gripping the soldier in her hand, Ellie went back inside and found her mom and Grandma sitting on the couch in the living room. Ellie's mom had the most beautiful material she had ever seen on her lap. The material was dark forest green with golden dragons and phoenixes dancing all over the fabric. She reached out her hand to touch it, but her mom stopped her.

"Go wash your hands first, sweetie."

Ellie ran to the bathroom and back. Grandma was telling a story about riding in a cart to a small shop where she had bought the fabric. Ellie touched the smooth silk. "What are you going to make?" She asked her mom.

"I haven't decided yet, but I'm thinking about making some pillows." Ellie's mom smiled at her. "Maybe if there's a little extra, you can make a small pillow for your doll." Ellie could hardly contain her excitement as she gazed at the beautiful fabric.

Ellie thought back to the years when she had longed to go to China. She had made the pillow, but constant use left the fabric faded and worn. As a child, Ellie had wanted to go to China to see and experience everything—the food, the sites, and the lifestyle. But as she got older, Ellie realized her dream to go to China was more about the people. She wanted to meet the people that her grandma had talked to. Even though she couldn't speak much Chinese, she wanted to know what those people were like.

People were starting to line up at the gate, and Ellie hurried to join them. Even though the "Now boarding" sign hadn't yet shown up, and she was pretty sure it would take a while for hundreds of people to get on the flight, she wanted to be ready.

An hour later, Ellie sat in her seat with a middle-aged American woman on one side and a Chinese man with glasses on the other side. A screen on the chair in front of her advertised *The Avengers*, and she licked around on the screen to see what movies they had, but mostly he couldn't stop thinking about how the world would look when he stepped off this plane. It would be afternoon when they arrived, and she would meet her new co-workers at the university where she would be teaching.

Once again, Ellie found herself wondering about everything from the language to the food to the weather. She had asked endless questions over email to one of the other American co-teachers who was living there, but she still felt completely unprepared. She tried to talk to the Chinese man beside her, but after his eyes wrinkled in confusion behind his glasses, he stammered, "My . . . English is poor."

"Oh, ok, no problem. I hope you have a nice flight!"

Ellie turned to the woman on the other side, but she had already opened a book and didn't look at Ellie when she tried to make eye contact. Instead, Ellie settled into her seat to think about her new life. Over the years, Ellie always begged her grandma to take her to Chinese restaurants, but Grandma usually refused. "You don't want to eat that American Chinese food. Wait 'till you can have the real thing, honey. It will be worth the wait."

And now here she was, just hours from her goal. *Would it be as fascinating as Grandma always said? Would it be too hot? Would her apartment be nice? Would the students listen to her during the English lessons?* A couple hours later, Ellie woke up and realized she had been sleeping. Her neck was bent sideways, and she tried to stretch out the kink. She looked at the map of the plane's progress. Already three hours, and it felt like they had just left. Only ten more hours to go!

Unable to fall asleep again, Ellie decided to watch a movie. After that, she dozed for a while. Surely, they were getting close now. Only five hours in. During the next movie, Ellie started to doze, but when she paused it to sleep, she couldn't move her legs into a position that was comfortable. The armrests seemed to be squeezing closer together, and the person in front of her had reclined the chair. Ellie longed to be able to stretch out her legs. *Good thing you aren't tall*, her brother had said. But at this point, Ellie realized that being short did not save her from the discomforts of airplane seats.

She pulled down the tray table and tried to lay her head on it, but the seat in front of her was so far back that trying to lay down caused her back to arch awkwardly. She put the tray table up and tried to finish the movie, shifting in her seat every few minutes. *Up* was supposed to be a great movie, why was it suddenly so boring? She gave up on the movie after a few more minutes.

Hoping to get up for a bathroom break, Ellie looked to her right, where the woman had her hands on the tray table, a mask over her eyes, and a neck pillow supporting her neck. Sleeping. She looked the other way, but the Asian man was also sleeping. Stuck.

Ellie checked the map. Only six hours in. Seven more hours. Not even halfway.

That's it, I'm going to be on this plane for the rest of my life. Thirteen hours is an eternity. Ellie covered her face and rubbed her exhausted eyes. She shifted in her seat and felt an uncomfortable object in her pocket. By this point, her pants had twisted around, and she didn't even know where her pocket was, but after some adjustments, she found the familiar form of the soldier. *Remember the dream.*

Ellie took a deep breath and stretched her feet as far as they could go, twisting her ankles under the seat in front of her. *This flight will end. It won't last forever, and then I can see the place I've dreamed about for so long.*

Ellie tried to picture her grandma on this plane next to her. But her grandma had told her flying back then was completely different. There had been no movies—Ellie tried to imagine how she would have survived the past nine hours without movies. Even though Grandma had said the seat areas were usually bigger, and she could stretch out her legs a little more, the plane was so noisy you wouldn't have been able to hear a movie anyway. But Grandma had said that the worst part was the smoke that snaked out from the smoking area.

For the entire flight, Grandma had endured the smell. Ellie breathed deeply. Yes, she would take a slightly more cramped seat in exchange for being able to breathe.

Ellie thought back to her grandma's adventures in China on that agricultural tour. As interesting as that sounded, Ellie was glad her adventures would revolve around teaching. Vising her grandparents' farm was fun, but nothing compared with the joy of seeing someone understand a new concept after you've explained it. Teaching was for her.

"But can't you teach here in America?" Ellie's best friend had asked her one day when they were talking about their plans for the future.

"I could . . . but . . . I just really want to go to China." Ellie answered.

"But, why?"

"I don't know. Ever since Grandma gave me that Terracotta Soldier and told me about the food and the people she met, I've wanted to go. She said the people are so kind, and even though they seemed poor, they were content with their lives. But they still worked super long hours because they hoped to make enough money to send their kids to a bigger city with better education."

"My parents worked super hard so I could get an education too. That's not so different."

"I know," Ellie struggled to find the words. "I just . . . I want to see something different. I want to see what their lives are like. I want to see what my grandma saw. She said the things she saw changed her life, and I want to get that perspective too. I want to understand their lives, and I want to learn something new. And who knows, maybe I can share a little bit of who I am with them."

"Well, just don't change too much without me."

"No promises, but you should come visit!"

"Maybe I can go with your grandma. She's the coolest grandma I've ever met."

"Yeah, no arguments there," Ellie laughed. "She's the best."

Ellie felt an ache in her heart. She was following the dream her grandma had given her—a dream to see new places and to meet new people, but now her grandma was far away.

Ellie spent the last four hours of the flight trying to sleep, trying to watch movies, trying to read, trying to eat, and trying to pray. Finally, the seatbelt sign came on, and the announcement told them to stay in their seats. The descent was agonizingly long, and after touching down, they taxied for another thirty minutes. But they were close. Ellie tried to see out the window, but the sleeping woman separated her from the tiny hole that led to the beautiful world outside.

The seatbelt sign dinged, and people crowded into the aisles. Ellie maneuvered her suitcase out of the overhead bin and plodded toward the door. She tried to smile at the flight attendants, but she mostly just wanted to get off the stuffy plane. The airport looked the same as any American airport until she got inside. The terminal was swarming with people! *I guess I shouldn't be surprised. A country with a population of 1.4 billion people is bound to feel different.* She headed toward the baggage claim with the rest of the people from her flight. They had arrived. She was in China, in this city she could barely pronounce. Ellie looked up to see a giant, life-size replica of the Terracotta Soldier in her pocket standing proudly in the terminal. Time for a new adventure.

Just One More Minute of Studying

Xueqing

Inspiration Words: AirPods and Milk tea

Wang Xueqing (wahng ssee-yoo-eh cheeng) stared at the pile of books on her desk. Then she turned around to look at the clock on the wall at the back of the classroom: 9:15 p.m. In forty-five more minutes, they could return to their dorms and go to sleep. The fluorescent lights shone a cold, white light throughout the room, and Xueqing looked out the window at the night sky that was already black. No moon tonight.

As Xueqing's gaze drifted from the window back to the classroom, she noticed her teacher looking in her direction. When they made eye contact, her teacher motioned for her to keep her eyes on her work. Xueqing turned back to the math textbook that was open in front of her. In the past twenty minutes, she had only completed three problems.

Studying for one more minute means that your future husband will be different. Xueqing's mom's voice echoed in her head. This was her mom's favorite thing to tell her to make her study, but Xueqing hated it when her mom said that. Of course, she didn't want to marry some bum from the village, but she also hated studying. And she definitely hated studying for twelve hours a day.

As these thoughts whirled around in her head, Xueqing caught the eye of her friend Dai Lin (die leen), who sat to her left. Dai Lin nodded in the direction of another classmate in front of them, and Xueqing stifled a giggle when she noticed that the other classmate was starting to nod off at his desk. His pencil had fallen out of his hands and his head was drooping forward.

But really, isn't that what we all want to do? Xueqing tried to focus her eyes on the math problems that still lay unanswered, but out of the corner of her eye, she saw the teacher pause her patrol to wake the dozing classmate. Even though she felt sorry for him, she didn't dare raise her head to observe the confrontation, and instead kept her eyes glued to the next math problem.

Halfway through the next problem, she noticed her foot tapping to an invisible beat and realized the melody to Eason Chan's (chahn) recent hit was running through her mind. *If only I had my AirPods, this study hall would be a million times more bearable!* Xueqing continued moving her foot in time with the imaginary music and tried to return to the math problem.

Five minutes later, Xueqing realized her pen wasn't moving, and she had been dreaming of her bed. No—she had been dreaming of a cold milk tea with those exploding tapioca beads full of fruity flavors. Just last weekend, she had managed to escape her practice tests long enough to go to the mall with a couple of her friends, including Dai Lin. They had walked slowly past the shops, laughing at the college girls snapping selfies with their expensive milk teas; all the while secretly wishing they were allowed to wear make-up at school and could afford to take selfies at the trendy milk tea shops, rather than the little outdoor stalls near campus.

I wish we could be in the mall now with some cold milk tea—even if it's cheap. Xueqing saw that her teacher was on the other side of the room and risked another look at the clock. 9:35 p.m. Twenty-five more minutes. She set her pen down and rubbed her eyes.

Twenty-five minutes plus six months. Then she would take the college entrance exam—then she could finally relax. She could go shopping whenever she wanted, and she could sleep whenever she wanted. If she could just survive the rest of this year, maybe life would get better.

Xueqing decided to give up on math for the time being. *Maybe if I take a break, I'll be able to study harder tomorrow.* Just one more minute of studying felt impossible, even if it did mean she would marry a bum. She started doodling an anime character with dramatic clothes and jagged hair. Smiling, she drew him a little cup of milk tea.

Watching Change
Old Woman

Inspiration Words: Metal and Coin

The old woman walked slowly toward the piles of vegetables in the wet market, her empty metal basket clattering over the brick sidewalk as she pulled it behind her. Once inside, she picked through the piles of green vegetables, making sure to choose the freshest ones.

Even at 7 a.m., the July heat outside was stifling, but even without air conditioning, the dark interior of the wet market remained semi-cool.

"Mom, I could really go shopping for you," the woman's daughter-in-law had said that morning while trying to distract her two-year-old with a toy truck. "It's awfully hot outside."

The woman knew her daughter-in-law didn't really want to go to the wet market, and besides, she enjoyed the walk. "No. You don't know how to choose the fresh vegetables. The ones you come back with always smell bad."

The old woman carefully chose her vegetables, putting them into the dented tin bowl that the owner of the small stall handed her. The woman barely looked away from her phone that was playing a dramatic scene from a TV show, and the older woman thought about the lack of service among the younger generation.

After she had chosen a collection of leafy green vegetables, some dirt-covered potatoes, tomatoes, onions, and an assortment of other colorful vegetables, the owner paused her TV show so she could weigh the items on a scratched, dirty scale. She mumbled numbers to herself while she added the prices together, but the old woman stopped her to ask about the price of the cucumbers.

"Oh, those are three yuan per *jin* (half a kilogram). Do you want some?" She passed the dented metal bowl back to her. The old woman added a few cucumbers and passed the bowl back. Instead of trying to count up all the prices in her head again, the vegetable stall owner reached for a calculator and began punching in the numbers as she re-weighed the vegetables.

"Altogether, the price is 18.8 *yuan (Chinese currency)*." She began putting the vegetables in small plastic bags, although her focus had returned to her TV show.

The old woman reached into a small pouch that she kept in her pocket and pulled out a twenty-yuan bill. She handed it to the woman, who paused when she saw the crumpled bill. "I don't have any change for you," the owner said.

"What do you mean, you don't have any change?"

"We don't keep much small change around here because everyone uses online payments these days." The woman motioned to the green and blue QR codes taped to the overhanging part of her food stall. "The change would only be one *yuan* and two *mao* (one tenth of a yuan), do you want to just forget about it?"

"I'm not going to forget about it! You ought to give me my change."

"I'm sorry, *ayi* (ah yee; a term meaning *aunt*, but used to address people older than yourself), but I really don't have any cash here. I can give you a discount next time!"

The old woman crossed her arms and glared at the younger woman.

"Ming Hao (meeng how), do you have a couple yuan I could borrow? I need 1.2 yuan." The younger woman shouted over to the owner of a nearby stall, who grunted and handed over a slightly-damp yuan bill and two small, silver coins.

Two other people had chosen and paid for their vegetables before the old woman finally had the proper change returned to her and had securely locked the bill and coins in her worn wallet. The stall

wner was back to watching her TV show by this point and barely
ooked up when the old woman picked up the bags of vegetables
nd deposited them in her metal basket as she headed to the dry
goods stall.

The stall was owned by a woman about her age, and the old woman
vas relieved to realize that this next stall would be okay if she paid
n cash. Maybe one day she would have to use that ridiculous online
payment, but she was going to put it off as long as possible, no matter
how much her son and daughter-in-law pestered her about the inconvenience she caused. Who knows what would happen to all their
money if they kept it all in some obscure online account? Besides, those
QR codes were so complicated to figure out. No, this way was better.

M&M's and a Holy Night

Ashley

Inspiration Words: Sneakers and M&M's

Ashley hurried into class on Tuesday, December 1st. Several students were already at their desks listening to music or extra English exercises, but the students started putting away their headphones when Ashley wished everyone good morning. Sunny and Candy smiled and returned the greeting. Several other students didn't lift their heads from their desks. As students drifted into the classroom, Ashley took out the textbook and began writing some vocabulary words on one side of the chalkboard.

She kept her coat on, and most of the students did as well. The air was chilly and damp. The floors of the building were slick with water, even though it hadn't rained last night—benefits of living in a tropical environment where humidity made the tile floors and walls drip with condensation. Ashley walked over to a few students and began asking them about their weekend.

"I just stayed in my dormitory and slept all weekend," Candy giggled as she answered the question.

"Yeah, I didn't want to go out, but yesterday, I went to the library to study," Sunny answered.

"Wow, sounds like a relaxing weekend!" Ashley smiled at the two girls.

The bell rang, and Ashley returned to the front of the class. "Good morning, everyone! And happy December!"

"Good morning," the students replied. This class was full of energy, and Ashley enjoyed interacting with them. Even though she wasn't an experienced teacher, the students always responded well to her lessons, and she looked forward to this particular class each week.

After class, Ashley walked carefully out of the building. The floors were still slippery, and the last thing she wanted was to land on her backside in front of all of her students. She wouldn't be able to live that down if that happened.

December 1st. Christmas is 25 days away. The midday sun had chased away some of the morning chill, and Ashley took off the scarf and stuffed it into her teaching bag. *Twenty-five days till Christmas, and there's not a speck of the season anywhere around here.*

According to tradition, Ashley and her American colleague had put up a Christmas tree with a few friends. They played Christmas music, forced the students to watch "How the Grinch Stole Christmas," and drank hot chocolate with the air conditioning on. The weather jumped back and forth between cold, hot, and wet so often that Ashley had a hard time figuring out what to wear, let alone what holiday feelings she was supposed to have.

She wanted to feel more in the holiday spirit, but the school buildings didn't have any Christmas decorations, and the only time she heard Christmas music was in the supermarket, where they played a children's version of "Jingle Bells" and "We Wish You a Merry Christmas." On repeat. After about five minutes of grocery shopping, Ashley could never stand it and usually put in headphones to instead listen to some Chris Tomlin songs.

If only I had some M&M's. Ashley thought back to Christmas in America. She thought of the chilly days in Pennsylvania. She thought of ice skating and cute hats and warm coats. And she thought about the bowl of M&M's that her mom always kept on the kitchen table throughout the month of December. These M&M's were the one treat they never had to ask permission to eat. Every morning, the bowl was always full—magically refilled from yesterday's snacking. Ashley and her brothers had theories about how many M&M's their parents would eat after they went to bed, but the most important thing was that there was always plenty for everyone. Ashley and her brothers used to sit around the table eating M&M's and talking about what they thought their parents might get them for Christmas that year.

But Ashley hadn't been able to find any M&M's on the school campus. There were some in town, but she hadn't had the chance to make the hour-long journey yet, so December was passing slowly, like any other month—without M&M's. Ashley tried to overlook the tacky Santa Claus stickers in the restaurant windows that only served to remind her that Christmas in China looked nothing like Christmas in America. Instead, she created her own Christmas environment at home at the end of the day, turning off all the lights but the twinkling lights on her Christmas tree, and one lone lamp on her coffee table Then, she would sit under the warm glow of the lamp with a good book and a cup of hot chocolate, leftover from the Christmas decorating party. Christmas was about Jesus' birth, of course, and Ashley tried to focus on that, but she still missed the beautiful neighborhoods with houses covered in Christmas lights and the holiday spirit glimmering in the shops in America.

Several days before Christmas, Ashley had finally finished her Christmas shopping and was trying to get ahead on her lesson plans so she could enjoy the one-day holiday the school gave her. She was excited to celebrate Christmas with a group of American friends who lived in the city. They planned to exchange gifts and cook together, just like they had for Thanksgiving. It wasn't quite the same as being in America with her family, but after all of her adventures with these people, they were starting to feel like family. Only a couple more days until Christmas Eve! Then, she could indulge in all things Christmas until she had to come back to school. She was already planning on staying as late as possible on Christmas Day so she wouldn't miss any of the festivities.

Ashley's phone buzzed, jerking her back to the present from her Christmas fantasies, and she checked the message: *Dear Ashly, we look forward to your attendance at a Christmas party the school will hold on December 25th. There will be a performance, and we hope you will be able to sing a song.*

Ashley stared in shock at the message. She barely noticed that they had misspelled her name because she was so stunned they would expect her to attend a performance on Christmas Day. Maybe they were just trying to include her in their Christmas celebrations, but Ashley had no desire to go to a Christmas performance where she would feel more like a display piece than an honored member. Besides, that meant she would have to give up celebrating Christmas with her friends in order to perform. And she would much rather spend Christmas Day actually celebrating Christmas, instead of attending a Chinese talent show masquerading as a Christmas party. No. Absolutely not. She was not giving up the one day she'd been looking forward to all month.

Ashley wanted to throw her phone across the room, but she managed to remember that Jesus wanted her to love these people, and their unawareness about her personal holidays and traditions shouldn't drive her to anger. She set the phone on her desk and walked into the living room to look at the Christmas tree. After praying about how to respond, Ashley picked up her phone again and typed a reply. *Unfortunately, I won't be able to make it on the 25th because that is Christmas Day. If you change the performance to December 23rd or 26th, I will be able to join.*

Ashley's next thought was to choose a Christmas song she would sing, in case she was required to perform and give up her holiday. She didn't mind singing, as long as the performance wasn't on Christmas Day, but what could she sing that would be beautiful and still communicate the truth that she loved about Christmas? Definitely not Jingle

Bells. Maybe something like "O Holy Night." Her phone buzzed again, with the school confirming that the performance would be held on December 23rd. In two days.

On the night of the performance, Ashley walked into the small auditorium, and her students ushered her and her colleague to some seats in the center. They waved at some students they recognized further down the row. Moments later, the performance began. Even though the performance was called a Christmas concert, the stage decorations were mostly pink and silver balloons with various colored lights that flashed up and down the stage. The songs were a variety of pop songs chosen by students. A group of girls performed a dance in black shirts and pants; black sneakers completed the look. The heavy beat tried to make Ashley forget it was Christmas, but she refused to forget.

After half a dozen singers, two more dances, and a couple of comedic skits Ashley didn't really understand, because they were

ompletely in Chinese, a couple of students came to where Ashley vas sitting and told her she should go backstage to get ready. Her olleague followed with a folder of the piano music, and when it was heir turn, someone pushed a grand piano onto the stage. Ashley valked out to the center of the stage with a microphone in her hand. The auditorium erupted into welcoming applause, and she smiled at ler students while the familiar opening chords echoed throughout he auditorium. The whispering stopped, and Ashley saw dozens of tudents recording with their phones as she began singing. "O holy light, the stars are brightly shining . . ."

By the time she got to the chorus, students had turned on the flash-lights on their phones and began waving them in the air in time with he music. She closed her eyes and felt Christmas entering into a small part of campus. She couldn't bring all the lights and cold weather to his tropical climate, but she could bring a small piece of Christmas nto this performance right now. She closed her eyes, blocking out the garish balloons and flashing lights—everything except for the piano nd her own voice. "Fall on your knees, Oh hear the angel voices, O light divine, O night, when Christ was born . . ." Ashley sang the vords, reminding herself that the most important part of Christmas vas having the chance to share God's love with these students that he loved so much. *Truly, He taught us to love one another. His law is love, and His gospel is peace.* That's why He came that holy night. To share His ove with others. M&M's and Christmas decorations and the beauty of the Christmas season all paled in comparison with this truth, and Ashley focused all of her energy on those words as the song finished.

Beach Dreams

Xueqing

Inspiration Words: Canvas and Daydreaming

Wang Xueqing (wahng ssee-yoo-eh cheeng) pulled the easel out from where she had stashed it between her bed and her roommate's bed and put a new canvas on the stand. She had only been able to afford a small canvas, but it was enough. She opened a few paints, humming as she began to mix them. A small fan spread hot, sticky air throughout the dorm room, and a fly flew through the open window. Although the room had an air conditioner, the girls only used it at night so they could save money. Xueqing's roommates were probably at the library where they could get free air conditioning, but she felt that deep, familiar longing to paint.

Sweat had beaded on her face by the time she finished mixing the paints and began painting her daydreams onto the fresh canvas. She spread out the clear blue sky, then tall sticks that pretended to be trees, with palm branches that offered little hope of shade waving in the breeze. A few round coconuts high above the ground completed the palm trees. She painted the sand stretching out along the bottom of the canvas and the ocean's white capped waves chasing each other towards the shore.

Spoken English class had been confusing as usual, and she preferred to spend class time daydreaming about the next scene she would paint. Coming to Hainan Island with these clear blue skies and a wide ocean had been her one consolation when her parents refused to let her attend art school. But she wasn't allowed to leave campus during the week, and on the weekends, her roommates were too "busy" to go to the beach, where they risked their skin getting even the tiniest bit darker. In the middle of campus, there was a large hole in the ground next to signs with conceptual pictures of the beautiful lake it would one day become. She hoped they would finish it soon, so at least she could enjoy a bit of water on campus. Until then, she would have to venture outside campus whenever she could to find some inspiration.

She had finally convinced a classmate, Kun Na (koon nah), to go to the beach with her last weekend, and they had taken a three-wheeled cart that felt like it might fall apart as it bounced over pot-holed roads. Conversation was impossible as the motor screamed, but thankfully, they only had to endure the bumps and the noise for about twenty minutes before they gave the driver fifteen *yuan*, and he parked next to some other three-wheeled vehicles to smoke and rest with his feet in the air.

Xueqing barely noticed what the driver was doing as she hurried towards those warm sands with her new friend. They had spent the afternoon in the shade, enjoying the breeze and the view. The coconuts were overpriced at nine *yuan*, but they had each bought one anyway and sipped them while they sat on a blanket. That view had inspired her daydreams in class, and now she was determined to paint it.

As the beach took shape under her guidance, Xueqing thought back to her English class. She usually tried to hide in the background, but today she had been unable to escape her teacher.

"Why did you choose to be an English major?" her teacher had asked. *Kun Na had helped to translate the question when Xueqing couldn't decipher the meaning. The teacher spoke with kindness and genuine curiosity, but Xueqing hadn't*

missed the irony of the question. Xueqing knew her English was terrible. In three weeks of class, she had only managed to embarrass herself with her ineptitude, and now the teacher was standing next to her desk, asking her what she was doing here. Xueqing wondered why she had chosen this major as she struggled to think about how to express herself. She finally just tried to tell the truth.

"My grades in the other subjects weren't good enough to study anything else." Kun Na had helped her to complete the sentence when Xueqing struggled to find the right words. After they had finally helped their teacher to understand the answer, Xueqing looked away. How stupid she must seem. Her English was so terrible, but somehow it was her best subject. She hadn't scored high enough on any of her other subjects to test into another major. Why did she choose to be an English major? Well, it was because she had no choice.

She wanted to explain that she loved art, and her dream was to be a painter, but her parents wouldn't let her paint because that kind of living was too uncertain. But how did she explain that to her teacher?

The teacher smiled kindly and said, "Well, I'm glad to have you in my class." She then moved on to another student and asked about his weekend plans.

Remembering the conversation made Xueqing blush again, even though no one was around. How was she ever going to survive four years in this impossible major? She finished the painting with a fluffy white cloud above her ocean and decided that maybe she could start by giving her paintings English names. This one would be *Beach Dreams.*

The Cold Shoulder

Chenrui

Inspiration Words: Delete and Cold shoulder

Ye Chenrui (yeh chun ray) slurped the noodles in a corner of the cafeteria, a TV show he had been interested in playing on his phone. The lead actor and actress were in the middle of a fight, but Chenrui knew they would end up together in the end. TV shows are like that: fight, fight, fight, until they finally stop fighting and end up happily together. *How come real-life friendships aren't like that?* He asked himself. *How come I don't know the end of this story? I'm not even asking for a girlfriend; I just want a friend who doesn't ignore me when I want to hang out.*

Chenrui wiped his forehead with a sleeve of his white shirt. Sweat speckled the rest of his shirt. This was his favorite one because it had the English word, *delete*, with a line through the word, emphasizing the meaning. He liked it because it made sense, unlike the English words and phrases many of his friends wore on their shirts.

As he looked at the sweat spots, he wondered if maybe he should have taken the noodles back to his dorm instead of trying to eat in the oven known as the cafeteria. Thankfully, the building was at least covered, but there was no air conditioning. The only relief came from the huge windows that were always open, but today, there was no wind. It was May, well into the summer weather, even though he still had two months left of classes. The cold noodles did little to ease the discomfort of the heat, and Chenrui tried to eat faster.

When he heard voices of people walking past him, Chenrui glanced up and saw his best friend talking and laughing with a group of his classmates. Chenrui immediately looked back at his TV show and wished he hadn't looked up. His friend had ignored him, but Chenrui knew he had noticed him. How could he not? His best friend had ignored his message so he could eat with those people for lunch. Betrayal crushed his heart while the heat pressed down on him, and he wondered if he would suffocate inside this airless building.

Back in his dorm room, Chenrui tried to take a nap, but he couldn't sleep. He kept waiting for the door to open, and his friend to walk in. *What will I say to him? Should I confront him, or just pretend I didn't see him?*

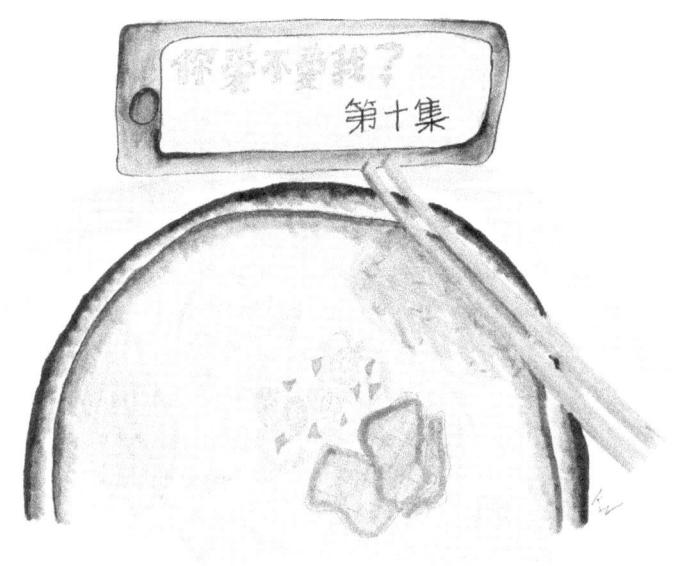

Should I ask him what he did for lunch and why he didn't answer my message, or should I just pretend nothing happened? Anger still burned inside him, and Chenrui knew if his friend came back now, he would probably just shout at him. *Where is he anyway? We don't have class this afternoon; why isn't he back in the room? I doubt he's in the library. Even when we were close friends, I couldn't drag him there.*

He finally gave up on the attempt at sleep and climbed down the side of the bed to the desk underneath the bed. He sat on the hard-backed chair and pulled one of his English books off the shelf. He opened up a file of his listening homework on his computer and began listening to the passage about whales. When the passage ended and he looked down at the questions, he realized he hadn't heard anything and would need to listen again. *Come on, Chenrui. Just let it go and focus on this listening exercise.*

After an hour of nearly worthless studying, the door opened and Ze Kai (zuh kie) walked in. Chenrui looked up at him and hoped that Ze Kai could see the anger in his eyes, but Ze Kai didn't even look at him as he grabbed a book, shoved it in his bag, and headed back outside. Neither boy spoke a word, and Chenrui's anger increased. He stood to chase Ze Kai down and confront him, but the thought of facing him in the hallway in front of countless watching eyes pushed him back into his seat. This didn't need to be more public than it already was. He would just return coldness with more coldness.

In class, Chenrui started sitting by himself, and he refused to work with his classmates when teachers asked them to work with partners or in small groups. As he sat looking at the books in class, he found he was able to focus less and less on the assignments. When he didn't participate, his teachers started avoiding him and stopped calling on him as much. When he saw Ze Kai working happily in a circle of talking classmates, Chenrui tried to focus on the words in front of him, but they blurred as anger consumed his thoughts.

One day after his marketing class, Chenrui packed up his books lowly. He usually took his time so he wouldn't have to walk out with his other classmates, but this time, his teacher came up to him.

"I've noticed that you don't seem very focused lately, Chenrui."

"Mmm." Chenrui didn't want to be rude, but he didn't know how to respond. He definitely didn't want to share his pain with his teacher.

"It's important to remember that you can't let outside things influence your studies. Your grades are very important, and your participation in class has been suffering lately."

"Yes, sir."

"You have potential to do some great things, and I'd hate to see that potential wasted. Let me know if there's anything I can do to help."

The teacher walked back to the front of the classroom, and Chenrui made a break for the door. "Ok," he mumbled as he left.

On his way to dinner, Chenrui thought about his teacher's words. *Maybe this was affecting him too much.* He and Ze Kai had been close for a semester and a half, but maybe it was time to move on. *But how do I stop being angry at him? He's such a jerk!* Chenrui walked on for several more minutes, reminding himself of all of the horrible things Ze Kai had done and all of the times his friend had ignored him. They didn't even talk in their dorm room anymore.

Maybe I could talk to him. The thought came, and Chenrui immediately wanted to banish the idea. *Never. Not until he apologizes to me. But . . .* Chenrui thought about his teacher's words. *Is this really worth hurting my grades? Maybe not.*

That night, Chenrui sat at his desk, once again waiting for Ze Kai to come in, but this time, he was planning out how to talk to him. *First, ask him why he started ignoring me—especially that day he ignored my message so he could eat with those other people.*

The door opened and Ze Kai came in. Chenrui took a deep breath and turned to him. "Why have you been ignoring me?"

Ze Kai had been turning toward his own desk, but at Chenrui's voice, he stopped abruptly and turned to him. "I've been ignoring you?" The surprise and anger in Ze Kai's voice startled Chenrui, but he refused to back down.

"Yeah," he stood to face his roommate. "When I asked you to go to lunch, you never answered, and then you went with our other classmates."

"You never asked me to lunch! *You've* been ignoring me for weeks now!"

Chenrui nearly stopped in surprise, but the anger he'd been holding inside for so long convinced him Ze Kai was playing innocent and lying to him. He whipped out his phone and found the message, the last one he had sent to Ze Kai. "See!" He challenged.

Ze Kai took a step closer to look at the message before pulling out his own phone. "I never received it. Look at my phone. It's not here." Ze Kai found the chat and held his phone out toward his roommate.

Chenrui glanced at the phone. Ze Kai was right. The message wasn't there. "Then why did you ignore me when you came back to our room?"

"Every time I come in here, you're studying and don't seem to want to be bothered. Why are you acting like a moody girl? Give me a break."

A moody girl? What a stupid thing to say! Chenrui searched for an appropriate response, but what was he supposed to say? Ze Kai was treating him like a child. "I can't believe you're treating me like this!" He finally said, stomping toward the bathroom.

"Treating you like what?" Ze Kai asked, following him, and stopping him outside the bathroom door. "It was just a misunderstanding."

"It was a misunderstanding because you didn't care enough about us to make it right."

Ze Kai rolled his eyes. "Come on, man." He punched Chenrui's shoulder just like he had the time Chenrui got second place in the speech competition. "Let's just forget about it. It's over, ok?"

For a moment, Chenrui thought about holding on to the anger. He didn't want to just let it go. Ze Kai was wrong. He had let this continue or weeks. He hadn't done anything to make it right. He was wrong.

Or maybe it was just a misunderstanding.

Chenrui turned away from his friend. He clenched his hands into fists. Then he unclenched them. He looked back at Ze Kai who still stood next to him. *We used to be best friends. Is it worth it to give that up because of a stupid text message that wasn't received?*

Chenrui let out a long breath. "Ok, yeah. Just forget about it."

When they sat down to play a game on their phones together, Chenrui thought about the happy ending on his TV show. Maybe life had some happy endings too—they just didn't come within 30 minutes of the problem, and maybe happy endings required a little more work to actually happen in real life.

Meeting the Parents

Anne and Johnson

Inspiration Words: Prancing and Brunch

"Have some more, we have plenty!" Anne tried to smile as her boyfriend's mom heaped cow stomach and some other unidentifiable animal insides on top of her bowl of rice.

"It's okay; I can get it myself. Don't worry about me." Anne tried to decline the generous gift of what the woman viewed to be the choicest delicacies on the table.

"Don't be shy! Eat up!" The woman smiled.

Anne looked to her Chinese boyfriend, Johnson, for help (even though she used his Chinese name around his family, she still thought of him mostly by his English name), but he was distracted in a deep Chinese conversation with his dad about housing prices in the city. She caught fragments of the conversation, but not enough to be able to join in.

Anne smiled at Johnson's mom, who was watching her to see if she enjoyed the food. Anne picked up a piece of the stomach, which seemed like the safest option, and put it in her mouth. It was chewy, and she wasn't sure exactly when to swallow, so she decided to just swallow quickly. Johnson's mom looked away and started talking to her sister. Sure that no one was watching, Anne sneaked some of the intestines into Johnson's bowl—he would enjoy them more than she would.

She had thought brunch would be a safe choice to avoid food she wasn't quite used to, but apparently intestines are a menu option even at morning tea restaurants. She reached for a steamed bun that was decorated to look like a pig. This one was one of her favorite buns, since it was filled with a sweet sauce made from yellow beans and sugar. The whicker steamers in the center of the table were filled with a variety of both sweet and savory buns, She was glad to let everyone else eat pig stomach if she could fill her bowl with steamed buns.

"What's your job?"

Anne looked up at Johnson's dad, who had asked the question. She had just taken a bite of the bun, so she tried to chew and swallow quickly.

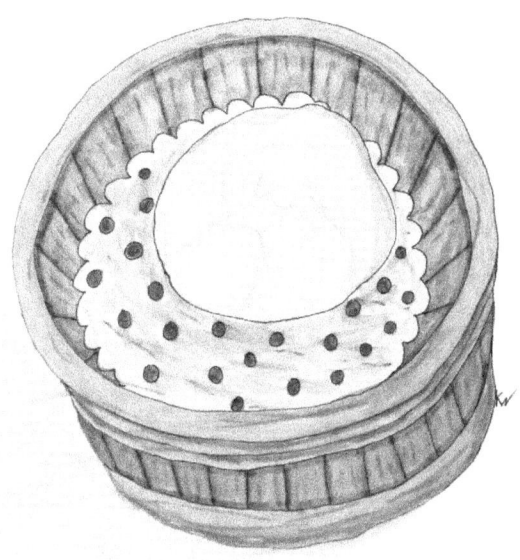

"She's a teacher," Johnson said, helping her out.

Anne finally swallowed, "Yeah, I teach university students."

"Oh, what subject do you teach them?" Johnson's mom asked.

"I mostly help my them prepare for the spoken English portion of the IELTS exam, since my students need a high score in order to go to England to continue studying."

"That's great! What a good job." Johnson's parents said.

"Johnson's sister is also a teacher, but she teaches kindergarten." Johnson's mom said.

"Oh, that's nice!" Anne smiled at Johnson's sister, who sat on the other side of the round table. "We'll have to share teacher stories later."

Johnson's parents asked her several more questions about her family and her time in China, and Anne was relieved she could understand most of what they said and answer all of the questions. The brunch seemed to be going well, which was a relief, since it was her first time to meet Johnson's parents. Well, what had started out as meeting his parents had turned into meeting his entire family, since Johnson's aunt, uncle, and their family, as well as Johnson's older sister, her husband, and her small daughter had also been invited.

Johnson's niece was currently prancing about the table in the private room, ignoring her mom's urging to eat some more noodles, another staple at Chinese brunch. The little girl wore a pink princess dress, and she seemed to be imagining she was at a ball in a castle, rather than at a brunch with her uncle's new foreign girlfriend. Anne smiled at the girl as she danced around the chairs. *She sure is cute! And she reminds me so much of my niece back home. I guess it's universal—no kid will choose sitting calmly in a chair for a meal over running around playing.*

Anne tried to eat slowly, making sure to always keep food in her bowl so no one would think she was going hungry and give her more food to eat. She tried to think of interesting things to say, and when Johnson's mom looked back in her direction, she was ready.

"There sure has been a lot of rain lately, wouldn't you say?" Anne asked.

"Oh, yes! Did you bring an umbrella today? It will probably rain this afternoon."

"Yes, I have my umbrella."

"Good."

"At this time of year, it's best to always keep an umbrella in your bag," Johnson's aunt joined the conversation.

"Yes, definitely," Anne agreed.

Anne's conversation skills failed her at this point. She always had a harder time being chatty when she was speaking in Chinese. Johnson leaned toward her and squeezed her hand under the table.

"You should ask my mom about her new dog!"

His mom heard the comment and immediately took out her phone, "You really have to see these pictures; he's absolutely adorable!"

Anne was thankful for the new conversation to keep all of their attention, and she smiled at Johnson before leaning over to look at the pictures and murmur her admiration of the fluffy, white dog. He really was cute—just a tiny puppy. "My family has a dog in America, and I remember when he was that small," she said. "When he was a puppy, he would sleep on my lap—now when I go back to America, sometimes he still tries to. I think he doesn't realize how big he is now!"

The rest of the meal passed smoothly, and when they finished eating, the family stood to leave. Anne smiled in relief, and also pleasure, at finally meeting these people who were such a big part of the man she was growing to know and care for. Their kindness was genuine, and even if Americans didn't usually show their welcome with cow stomach, Anne realized these people were quite similar to her own family.

"Goodbye!" Anne said at the entrance to the restaurant as she and Johnson headed toward the subway station and his parents, toward a bus stop.

Johnson's dad patted Johnson's shoulder in farewell.

"Have a good rest this afternoon," his mom said.

Anne smiled and waved. "Do you wanna have a video call with

my parents later tonight?" she asked as they walked away. "They're so much like your parents—I think you'll like them."

"Good idea," Johnson said.

The Soundtrack of My Life

Novel

Inspiration Words: Overhear and Acoustic

My primary skill in life is overhearing things. I don't talk much, but I listen plenty, and when I listen, I hear lots of interesting things. One of the first conversations I remember overhearing was between my parents. I was in my bedroom when they started arguing. I had been playing with my doll, imagining a conversation between us, but I put it down to listen to what my parents said. One of them wanted to eat at 5:30 p.m., and the other one insisted that 6 p.m. was just as good for eating dinner.

I looked at the clock by my bed: 6:05 p.m. I had already opened the door so I could hear the discussion clearly, and at first, I just stood there, expecting them to conclude that maybe the conversation could be finished after dinner. After two hours and a lot of tearful accusations, I sneaked into the kitchen, filled my plate with cold food, and took it back to my bedroom. I don't think my parents ate that night.

My dad moved to Beijing when I was in primary school, so I usually stay with my mom here in Guangzhou (gwohng joh). Now that I'm in college, I go to visit her several times a month. She doesn't talk as much as she used to, but I sometimes wonder if that's because I don't argue with her. We keep our conversations pretty basic. Dad comes back to visit sometimes, but I try to be busy those evenings. I've overheard enough arguments to be something of an expert on how they will end: with slammed doors.

Sometimes when I go to the mall, I overhear interesting conversations. Moms scold their kids; Grandmas chat about the weather or their most recent mahjong match. Boyfriends and girlfriends giggle about things, although those conversations tend to be too quiet for even me to overhear, so I'm never quite sure what they're giggling about.

My favorite conversations include foreigners. There are quite a few foreigners in Guangzhou, and I like to listen to things they say in order to practice my English. Sometimes I put in my headphones, and don't turn anything on so people won't bother me, but I can still listen to conversations around me.

One time, a little foreign boy with blonde hair and a round face pointed at an old Chinese man and said, "Mommy, look at the huge mole on that man's face. It's so black and has hairs coming out of it!" His mom tried to shush him, and her face turned quite red.

My roommates here at college call me Novel, (xiao shuo, ssee-ow hwoh), because although xiao shuo means "Novel" in Chinese, the characters also literally translate to "Little Speak." They joke that one day, maybe I will put all my thoughts into a novel—then everyone will finally know what I'm thinking. Maybe I will one day, or maybe that's what this is.

It's not that I don't like to talk; I think I've just decided that the things I have to say won't be appreciated by people who hear me. Maybe, deep down, I'm also a little afraid nobody will want to listen to what I have to say. It's easy to just keep my talking down to a minimum. Thinking is more interesting anyway.

I think sometimes my roommates forget I'm there and start talking about things that would make some people feel uncomfortable. But I've decided that I don't care. If they want to talk to their boyfriends about all manner of things while someone else is in the room, at least it provides an interesting soundtrack for my homework.

In the first week of class, I learned two things. First, I learned that the bathroom has great acoustics. Second, I learned that my roommate, Xiao Liu (ssee-ow lee-oo) really likes to sing in the shower. She's normally a little bit shy, but when she's in the shower, it's like she becomes another person, belting out Adele at the top of her lungs. I find it particularly ironic when she sings, "Hello from the other side," and in my mind, I answer her, "Yes, hello from outside of the bathroom, your personal concert stage."

After a life of few words, I have become fairly comfortable with myself and my habits. But yesterday, when I was lying on my bed, trying to doze during the hottest part of the afternoon, I realized not everyone was as comfortable with my habits as I was.

"It's just that she's so quiet," Duo Duo (dwoh dwoh) didn't exactly whisper to Xiao Lu.

I forgot about dozing and tuned in. Didn't they realize that just because I'm quiet doesn't mean I'm deaf? Oh well, it sounded like they were talking about me, and I wanted to know what they said.

"I'm quiet, too, around people I don't know." Xiao Lu answered in a lower voice.

"But I don't think I've heard her say three full sentences together. Doesn't that seem . . . I don't know . . . a little . . . strange?"

By the end of the conversation, I felt like both girls agreed I was "strange."

Great. Here I am, just trying to enjoy college and live my life, and now I'm strange. So, I'll do what I always do when people think I'm strange. I just stay quiet. Maybe if I stay quiet, then they will stop bothering me. If it works with my parents, maybe it will work with my roommates too.

Diary of a Language Learner

Becky and Samantha

Inspiration Words: Pandemonium and Confused

September 19th

This is my first week of classes at university, and I absolutely love it! I'm so glad I came to Hainan. The skies are so blue here, and even though it's so hot, the library has air conditioning, and that's basically where I spend most of my time anyway. I also just got a new umbrella, so I have constant sun protection. My new umbrella is yellow with little flowers on it, and it makes me happy because, even if I have to use it when it's raining, there's still a sun above me!

Actually, I have to say that the last couple of weeks were pretty awful. We had military training, and I cannot describe how hot it was. Our clothes were not designed for the long hours of standing in this unbearable sun. I know every college student has to complete a few weeks of military training, no matter what university you go to, but I wish it weren't mandatory, and I wish I knew why we all have to do it. Maybe it's just to teach us how to do hard things. Or teach us discipline. Whatever it is, I just wished we could skip past military training to start regular classes as quickly as possible!

After two days, one of my classmates passed out. We were all practicing marching, and she was not in time with the rest of us. She went to sit on the grass, but as soon as she sat down, she passed out. When I saw what had happened, I also realized I was starting to feel a little dizzy. We were allowed a water break while they took the girl to the campus doctor. She seemed fine later that evening, and now, they give us more water breaks, which is a relief. I'm really close to all of my classmates, and we all have a great relationship. Hey, maybe that's the point of military training! It shows us all how to work together and helps us make friends when we first come to college.

But I was thrilled when the three weeks of military training were over so I could start studying English! So far this week, I have had an English listening class, a comprehensive English class, a reading class, and a basic culture class.

I'm most excited for tomorrow, because tomorrow, I have my first ever class with a foreign teacher. After studying English for ten years, I will finally have the chance to practice with a real person—from another country! The class schedule says her name is SAMANTHA. I'm not sure how to say that name, and it seems very long. I wonder what I'm supposed to call her. Maybe I'll just call her teacher. That seems safe.

Well, I should probably go to sleep. Spoken English at 8:00 a.m. tomorrow morning!!!!

September 20th

What a day! Let me tell you, spoken English class was extremely interesting, but so different from what I expected. It started off okay; Teacher just told us her name and made us practice the "th" sound. Since most of us couldn't get it right, she said we could just call her Sam. But that was confusing when she found out that one of the boys in our class also chose "Sam" as his English name. So, she said we could call her Samantha and practiced the name a few more times. It's such a long name, though, so I think most of the students will just call her "Teacher."

She also told us about her family (she has so many brothers and sisters) and her hometown, but I couldn't understand most of what she said. I've been studying English for so many years, and I always get the highest score on my English tests—why couldn't I understand her? I really feel like I should be able to understand her better. I will have to practice more.

I talked to some of my other classmates, and I realized they were also completely confused. They didn't even seem to know she had explained the class rules to us. I couldn't understand what the rules were, but I know she mentioned something about rules. I hope I don't break any of them. Maybe I will ask her about them next time. She seems really nice, but I was a little afraid to talk to her because I was worried that I wouldn't understand what she says to me. Maybe I will try next week. She has such a nice smile, and such big eyes. We all noticed her big eyes. I don't think I have ever seen such big eyes in my whole life, and they're blue! Maybe she is a model back in America.

Samantha also made sure all of us had English names. I asked her to give me one, and she gave me a list of names. I chose Becky. Samantha said it's a good name, and it's also the name of her cousin! I have the same name with Samantha's cousin!

Twenty minutes before class ended, Samantha told us we were going to play a game. We all understood those words, and we got really excited! She gave us some paper and asked us to write the numbers one to fifteen down the left side of the page. She even showed us an example, so I think we all did it right. Then she put up so many words on the PowerPoint that everyone forgot we were supposed to be playing a game. It was so overwhelming!

After she explained the game, we realized what we were supposed to do. The PowerPoint had a list of fifteen descriptions. The first one said we should find someone who was wearing blue, and the second one was to find someone from Hunan Province. Each of the other numbers had different descriptions too. Once Samantha said, "Go!", we then had to walk around the room to find classmates who matched the description for each of the fifteen numbers. I was glad I spent so much time talking to everyone during the military training. I already knew my friend Ma Liang was from Hunan, and Yun Hong had a pet cat. Before the game had even started, I'd already found #2 and #7. I thought maybe I could be the first one to finish!

After just a few minutes, the entire classroom was in pandemonium! Everyone was shouting. I was trying to speak in English like Samantha asked us to, but it was so loud no one could understand what I was saying, so sometimes I just shouted the number and let the other person read the description for themselves. I found a girl who had visited Beijing, a guy who was good at singing, and another girl who had a part-time job during the summer holiday—all within the first minute or two. The classroom was also not very big, and we all got stuck between the desks as we tried to maneuver around the room. It got pretty tough to find the people I needed to talk to, but eventually I found people who fit all fifteen descriptions and gave my paper to Teacher.

Later, after everyone sat down, she announced that "Becky" was the first one to finish. At first, I looked around to see who that was— then I realized that I am Becky! I was the winner! I was so excited when everyone clapped for me. I absolutely love this class, and I really hope that next time I can understand what Teacher is talking about!

~Becky

Tacos and Cheese
Braxton

Inspiration Words: Tortilla and Aspirational

Braxton sat down on the hard chair in the dining room of his restaurant. It was 2 a.m., and the last of the night crowd had just left. The kitchen staff had finished cleaning up, and he had put away the rest of the drinks at the bar. As he drummed his fingers on the colorful Mexican tablecloth, Braxton checked the messages on his phone. He noticed a Chinese message that he had received at 10 p.m. from the police bureau. He sent it to himself in another app so he could translate it to English and read, *We have received more complaints about the noise level in your restaurant. Kindly remember to respect your neighbors.*

Without answering, Braxton set his phone down on the striped tablecloth. How had so few customers managed to garner such a complaint? He had almost gotten used to messages like this and the signs reminding customers to be quiet as they left. Why didn't the signs seem to make a difference to his complaining neighbors? *Sure, Grandma has to sleep, but if she closed her windows, maybe she wouldn't hear as much.*

Braxton tried to be understanding, but he was starting to feel the stress of the last couple of months. He had already received several similar messages, and he knew that perhaps his gentle warnings were coming to an end. *What would the police do if the neighbors continued to complain? What would happen to the life I've built?*

In the dim light of the restaurant, Braxton looked around at the yellow walls and the paraphernalia that helped to distinguish this restaurant from most of the Chinese restaurants in the area. Flags and postcards covered one wall. He looked at the red Chinese flag with those five yellow stars hanging next to the Stars and Stripes of America. Why was it so hard to be a foreigner in this country he loved?

"I just wanted to give you tacos and cheese. Who can resist something so good?" Braxton spoke the words aloud to the silent darkness. Surely Granny wouldn't hear him now.

Braxton thought of his foreign customers, the strangers who had become his friends. He thought about Danny from Arizona, who had finally convinced his Chinese wife that Tex-Mex burritos were not overpriced KFC wraps.

"Even the tortilla is different!" Danny had said pointing at the burrito while Braxton watched, smiling from the bar.

Danny had insisted his wife try a burrito. "Perhaps the ingredients are similar to those KFC wraps—all it has is flour and water, but it's so much thicker and richer!"

Danny's wife had smiled politely, but declined eating any more. Danny shrugged and finished the burrito himself. The couple came in several times over the years, and Danny's wife had finally started eating the burritos. After a time or two, Braxton noticed she had even started to enjoy them.

Braxton remembered the day she came in without her husband, but with a group of her Chinese friends instead. She had walked confidently into the restaurant and smiled at him as if she were a co-conspirator in a plot.

"Show them what Tex-Mex food is," she had said, as she paid for her friends' lunch.

But Danny and his wife had left for America eight months ago for a short vacation, right before Covid started. Once the coronavirus situation was less serious in China, Danny had been unable to return because the situation had worsened in America, causing China to close its borders to Americans. More than half of Braxton's customers had disappeared for the same reason. Some had left when the situation in China became unbearable with strict quarantine rules. Most of Braxton's neighbors hadn't left their house for three weeks during the worst of the situation (except to take out the trash—he had heard).

Now Braxton wasn't even sure he would be able to renew the license for the restaurant. This restaurant had been his dream. He loved the people who came. He loved the late-night crowd the most, especially on Taco Tuesday, when he offered a buffet of all-you-can-eat tacos. He loved trivia night, even though that had originally been his brother's idea. He loved seeing the excitement on people's faces throughout the evening. He loved everything about his shop. Was Covid-19 really going to cost him all of this? But what could he do?

"It's going to be okay. We'll figure something out," his wife had said the week before, when they talked about the business license problem.

But what if that "something" is going back to America? Braxton hadn't said it, but he knew it was looking more and more likely. Foreigners were disappearing from China, and even the ones who remained were often unable to go out with the same freedom as before. The virus was affecting everyone. He often walked down small side streets and saw "Last chance" sales for small shops that would soon be closing their doors.

When he first told his family about the restaurant, they had called him aspirational, and if he gave it up now, he knew he would feel lost. But what choice did he have?

Finally, Braxton stood, pressing against that colorful striped tablecloth as he rose. Maybe he would close his doors, but he still had a wife who would be expecting him home, and he didn't want to keep her waiting any longer.

Shopping Races
Anne and Johnson

Inspiration Words: Yes and Sidewalk

"Stop dawdling, Anne," her mother scolded her as they walked through the aisles of the supermarket.

Anne held gently to the side of the grocery cart, keeping close, like her mom preferred.

"Can you get some of the chocolate chips from that shelf near the bottom?" While Anne grabbed a bag of chips, her mom picked up a package of pretzels.

When they were in the grocery store, Anne felt like her mom was in a carefully planned battle. Every move was executed for the smoothest possible result, and she didn't like delays.

As Anne thought about her grocery store trips with her mom, she remembered the strategy her mom would remind her of in the car before they got out: *"Now remember Anne, we want to get in, get out, and get home as quickly as possible. Here's the list, so let's work together to make this trip smooth!"*

While her mom thought of it as a plan, Anne thought of it as a game. She liked games, and she imagined her mom and herself in a competition with the other shoppers. Once she thought of the idea of making it a game, she stopped dawdling and was quick to help her mom pick up things. Every time they arrived at the check-out line faster than the other people they had entered with, Anne gave them a winning score. According to Anne's record, their longest winning streak was that five weeks the summer before sixth grade.

Now that Anne lived in China, she didn't usually think of her supermarket runs as a competition. For one thing, there were too many shoppers to keep track of who entered and left at what times. But she still found her game was a good way to deal with the anxiety she felt walking into crowded Chinese supermarkets. Unlike back home, the aisles were always packed with people, and noise filled the building as people jostled for space to weigh their produce and workers shouted about new products to potential customers. And today, she would face the supermarket crowds with her new boyfriend, Johnson. They were supposed to buy some food to make dinner for themselves and another couple, who were supposed to arrive at 6 p.m. Johnson had agreed to cook Chinese food, and Anne couldn't wait to try the dishes he would make.

Three o'clock came and went, and Johnson still hadn't arrived at Anne's apartment. *Where are you?* She started to text him, then deleted it—she didn't want to be impatient. Instead, she picked up her book and tried to read a few more pages.

At 3:10, she checked the clock again. *Read your book.* She command-ed herself. *The supermarket is nearby. We still have plenty of time.*

Every five minutes, she glanced at the clock again, and at 3:30, she finally heard the expected knock on the door. Johnson came in, a bit sweaty from the short walk from the subway.

"Hi! You made it. Are you ready to go?"

Johnson took off his shoes, slipped into some house slippers, and headed to the bathroom to wash his hands. "Do you mind if I rest for a few minutes first?"

"Sure, go ahead." Anne glanced at the clock. A few minutes wouldn't matter. If they left at 4:00, they should be able to get into and out of the grocery store in an hour, leaving an hour to prepare the food.

At 4:00, they were both ready to leave, and they walked to the supermarket across the street. The sidewalk was crowded with Saturday shoppers popping in and out of the tea shops, nail salons, and small restaurants as they walked down the street.

"Are you sure you don't want to make a list before we get there? I'm afraid we might forget something." Anne looked up at him and started to pull out her phone, where she kept her own list.

"Nah, it should be fine. We can just see what we need when we get there."

"Okay . . ."

Once inside the building, Anne directed their steps to the top floor so they could work their way down. They walked past the dried squid and other seafood laid out in open bins. First stop was the produce area.

"Oh! Look at these grapes! They would be great to have after our meal." Anne put them into the basket Johnson carried. "What vegetables do we need?"

"Hmm, let's see." Johnson glanced around at the assortment of fresh vegetables displayed on tables around him. "Maybe some spicy peppers." He sorted through the peppers until he approved of four of them.

"Great! What's next?"

Johnson picked up some lettuce from the vast selection of green vegetables before moving toward the deli area. As he glanced over the packaged choices, he looked around. "Isn't there any meat that's already cut?"

"It doesn't look like it, and I don't see a worker in this area. Let's just get this one and cut it when we get home."

"You can cut it?" Johnson looked hesitantly at Anne.

"Sure, I mean, it's just meat."

"I just . . . I've never cut meat before."

"What?" Anne looked at her boyfriend, who still held the package

of uncut meat, and craned her neck to look again for any nearby workers. "It's fine. I can cut it if I need to. But maybe we should hurry a little bit. It's already 4:45."

Johnson meandered through the vegetables and ended up in the dry goods section before Anne realized they hadn't weighed and priced the vegetables. And surely, they needed something else besides just spicy peppers and lettuce?

"Why are we looking at the noodles? Don't you wanna finish getting the vegetables?"

"Oh, sure, we can do that. I just saw these noodles on sale over here. But I don't know which ones we should get."

"Let's decide *after* we get the vegetables."

When the rest of the vegetables were properly bagged, priced, and sealed, Anne directed their steps to the noodles. "All right, let's get these noodles quickly."

Selecting the noodles was not fast, and neither was the process of finding and choosing the right spicy sauce or finding the drink Johnson had been wanting to try.

Anne glanced at her watch. Already 5:10. *This was not going well! Maybe it will only take 30 minutes to cook all the food. I can cut the vegetables and meat, and if he cooks at the same time, we'll be done in time.*

As Anne directed their steps past the hand soap and laundry detergent, Johnson stopped at the toothpaste. "I was wanting to buy some new toothpaste. I'm gonna just see what they have here."

"But Johnson, we're going to be late. We have to hurry home and cook dinner, or everything will be a mess! I don't understand why this is taking so long. Can we *please* just go pay?"

"Oh ok, umm . . . sure." Johnson agreed, and they found a short checkout line. As they walked back home, Anne walked at a brisk pace, leaving Johnson to match her speed. She tried to remind herself that the night was going to be fine. *It doesn't really matter if we start dinner a few minutes late, does it?*

"Did you usually go shopping with your parents when you were younger?" she said in an attempt at conversation.

"Yes, usually we would go on Saturday. It was my favorite part of the week because I could spend time with my mom and dad and play with my sister. We didn't do a lot of things all together as a family, so this was special. We would go in the morning, and my sister and I would play in a special play area while my mom and dad did most of the shopping. Then they would pick us up, and we would help pick out the fruits and vegetables. It usually took all morning. Afterwards, we would go out for lunch together."

Anne slowed her pace and looked up at Johnson. "Oh, I see. So shopping was more of a fun family activity for you than a chore."

Johnson nodded.

She wanted to say something more because he didn't usually share memories like this with her. But she couldn't think of anything to say that would justify her pushiness in the store, so she just said, "Next time, we should go earlier so we can spend more time shopping together."

"Yeah, I'd like that."

Fishing

Xiao Lu

Inspiration Words: Egg Tart and Post

Xiao Lu (ssee-ow loo) licked the crumbs out of the aluminum wrapper that, moments before, had contained a tasty egg tart. Saturdays were his favorite. He said it was because each Saturday, his mom would buy him the egg snacks that he loved so much. Each egg tart was shaped like a tiny pie, with a flaky crust and a smooth and custardy filling. He did love them, but what he never admitted was the real reason for his love of Saturdays.

After he had finished licking the crumbs out of his wrapper, he looked toward the box in the center of the table. There was still one more egg tart in there.

"Don't even think about eating my egg tart, Xiao Lu." Wen Kai (wuhn kie), Xiao Lu's older brother, didn't look up from his phone. The battle that was raging under the control of his thumbs occupied most of his sight, but he spared a sliver of attention for the egg tart in the middle of the table.

"Are you ever gonna eat it?"

"Yeah."

"When?"

"When I'm ready."

"Ugh." Xiao Lu scooted off the chair that was just a little bit too tall for him and started to pick up a truck he had been playing with before the egg tarts arrived.

"Xiao Lu, go wash your hands before you play with your toys!" Xiao Lu's mom called from the kitchen where she was washing some fruit.

After rinsing his hands as fast as possible, Xiao Lu was back to his truck. "Dad, can we go to the park today?"

"Let me check the weather." His dad exited out of the news app on his phone and pulled up a weather report. "Looks good, let's do it!"

Xiao Lu jumped up and ran into his room. Seconds later, he returned with a fishing net and a small plastic box with clear sides so he could see the fish he would catch and put inside. "Ok! I'm ready!"

"Are you gonna come, Wen Kai?" Xiao Lu looked at his brother, who was still engaged in fierce combat on his phone.

"Wait. This is a good game. I've been recording it too, so after I finish, I want to post it on my TikTok. Let me win; then I guess I'll come."

"Hold on a few minutes, Xiao Lu. Your mom and I need to get a few things ready first."

Thirty minutes later, Xiao Lu jumped out of the car, hopped on his small red scooter, and started pushing himself toward the lake. This Saturday was going to be even better than normal.

For the rest of the morning, Xiao Lu stood in the mud and weeds at the edge of the lake, catching tadpoles and getting wet. His dad took him to another part of the lake that was too deep to get in, but they could see some bigger fish in the water.

Wen Kai spent most of the time on his phone because he had failed to win the game, and was still working to unlock the next level. But when they walked around the lake to the side with the bigger fish, even Wen Kai put away his phone long enough to join. "Wen Kai, your phone time is up for this morning. Put your phone away." A directive spoken by his dad might have had something to do with the change in focus.

Their mom spent most of the time on the picnic blanket, watching Xiao Lu and making sure he didn't get into any trouble. Xiao Lu made sure she was watching by going just a little deeper than he was supposed to, so he could hear her call him back. Then he went back to safer ground.

That afternoon, Xiao Lu's parents put on a movie for him, but he didn't want to watch it. He kept running into his parent's bedroom, where they were trying to take a nap. Finally, he convinced his dad to come into the living room with him. They sat on the long couch in front of the TV, but his dad didn't last very long before he fell asleep. Xiao Lu didn't mind. He put his little body next to his dad's and watched the rest of the cartoon.

At dinner, Xiao Lu didn't want to eat. He pushed his food around, knowing the end of his favorite day was coming. His mom coaxed some food into his mouth, and he ate it, but he still didn't try to eat by himself.

"Go put on your pajamas and brush your teeth," his mom said when she gave up on convincing him to eat anything else.

"Ok . . ."

"Goodnight, son. We'll have some fun again next weekend." Xiao Lu's dad smoothed his hair as Xiao Lu headed to the bathroom. He would leave for work the next morning before Xiao Lu woke up, and he worked such long hours that Xiao Lu rarely saw him for more than a few minutes throughout the week.

"Goodnight, Xiao Lu," his mom said from the other side of the table. "I just heard Grandma come in from her square dancing, so she'll be in in a few minutes to make sure you don't need anything before you fall sleep."

Xiao Lu was glad Grandma would be there tonight. She always knew why he was sad on Saturday night. At least Mom and Wen Kai would be there on Sunday before Wen Kai had to go back to school, and his mom would also go back to work. But Sundays just weren't as fun as Saturdays.

Life Meets Work

Paul

Inspiration Words: Balloon and Perplexed

Paul sat in the large, open office area at the training center. He leaned back in the chair, resting his head against the back, with his legs stretched out in front of him. Most of the lights were off, and a balloon drifted by in the light breeze made by the air conditioner. Somehow, the balloon must have wandered in from the main room where the party had taken place. He caught it when it brushed against one of his hands that were dangling down over the sides of the chair.

What a night. Paul thought. Since he had started working for the English training center (a company that offered extra English classes and activities for children and adults), everyone used Paul's English name so much he had started to think of himself as Paul rather than Fu Hao (foo how), his Chinese name.

As far as he could tell, the party had been a success—dozens of new students had come, and Paul had smiled and made small talk, making everyone feel important and excited. Paul had noticed that the students liked talking with him, and he had enjoyed all the attention. Maybe it was because of his height. Paul knew he was taller than most of his other Chinese co-workers, especially since he was in the South. Or perhaps they had noticed his handsome features and carefully styled hair. Paul had taken extra time to make sure that the gel he used in his hair was just perfect today. But he really hoped they enjoyed talking to him because he was so much fun to be around. He had made jokes, and everyone had laughed at all the right places. Whatever the reason, Paul relished the attention and was looking forward to working with any new students the event brought in.

Paul's phone buzzed on the table, but at first, he didn't notice he was receiving a call. Since the end of the party, his phone had been vibrating almost constantly with WeChat (a social messaging app) notifications from all the new students. He had been ignoring them for the past several minutes, enjoying the silent office. But once he realized it was a phone call instead of more messages, he checked the caller and saw that it was one of his best friends, Cai Ling (tsie leeng).

"Hey, Cai Ling! What's going on?" He said as he answered the phone.

"Where are you? Why haven't you answered any of the messages in our group? We all had dinner and now we're having some drinks, and we thought you were going to come!"

Paul put the phone on speaker so he could scroll through his messages while he listened to her. There, he found the messages in their group chat with some of his closest friends from university. "Oh no, I just saw your messages. I thought I mentioned that I would be at a party for my new job at the training center. We just finished."

"Well, you definitely didn't say anything about that to us."

"Oh, oops."

"You could come over now? We'll probably be here for a while still."

Paul glanced at the time on his phone. "It's already 11 p.m., and I have to work tomorrow."

"Tomorrow is Saturday!"

"Yeah, at training centers, the weekends are the busiest, so I have to work all day tomorrow and Sunday."

"Ahh, well, sounds like we won't be seeing you much."

"Listen, I'm sorry I can't join you tonight, but I really need this job. You know I've been looking for a job for a long time, and now I finally have one. Can't you be happy for me?"

"We are happy for you, right, guys?" A chorus of agreement sounded over the phone, and Paul realized she had put him on speaker. "Didn't we have dinner to celebrate your new job last week?"

"Yeah, and now I have to work according to their times, which unfortunately, are opposite from your work schedules. But I'm gonna still hang out with you all. I'm just completely exhausted tonight. How about next week?"

"Ok, no problem, man." Several of the guys echoed the sentiment before Paul hung up.

I really should go home. This is gonna be a long weekend.

Six Months Later

Once again, Paul sat in the office under the dimmed lights, having collapsed into his chair. They had just finished the Christmas party, and Paul laughed again as he thought about their parody skit of *Home Alone*. Until this year, he'd never even seen the movie, but one of the foreign teachers at the center had suggested it for the party. All of his students had done a great job, and he was so happy when his boss complimented him on the participation of his students.

But the best part was when they begged him to sing a song. Everyone had screamed and cheered, and it had been perfect. Being here made him feel like a movie star. Everyone loved his classes, so he had been trusted to teach more and more of them. Last month, his boss had given him the teacher of the month award, and Paul hadn't stopped smiling for the rest of the week.

As he reclined in the chair, he scrolled through WeChat posts, looking at all his students' posts from the evening. He smiled when he saw the selfies he had taken with many of the students. Then, in the middle of posts of students dressed in reds and greens, he saw a group of people at a restaurant. Those were his friends. Why hadn't they invited him to join them? Why were they hanging out without telling him?

This is ridiculous. How can I be so popular here at work, and my own friends don't even want to hang out with me anymore? He scrolled through the unread messages on his phone. Nope. No invitation. Paul found the picture again and stared at it, perplexed. Yep, everyone was there except him. Had they made a new chat group without including him? That's ridiculous! How could they be so exclusive?

Paul began composing a scathing attack on the heartlessness of his friends as he searched for that group. He found it and was about to start typing when he paused—300 unread messages. He scrolled through the messages and realized they had invited him, but he had put the group on mute because he kept getting notifications during his class, and he really couldn't be disturbed. Oops.

Paul put the phone down. No wonder they had stopped calling him. He hadn't hung out with them in two months.

He picked up the phone again and called her. "Cai Ling?"

"Who is this?"

Paul grimaced. She either hadn't checked the caller ID, or she was trying to put him off.

"It's me, Paul."

"Oh, hey. Nice party. I saw your post."

"Thanks, I saw your post too. Are you guys still hanging out tonight?"

"Yeah, but don't you have class tomorrow?"

"I do, but if you guys will be there for a while, send me the location, and I'll be there as soon as I can."

"Great! See you soon!"

Paul smiled, gave himself a spritz of cologne, and left the nearly empty training center building.

No Pain No Gains (Another Diary of a Language Learner)

Becky

Inspiration Words: Trying and Potential

September 6th

Well, here we are, about ready to start another semester! I love the beginning of the semester. Having a long summer holiday is always fun, but going back to school with all those new books and new classes is the best. I'm also so happy to be with my roommates again! We had a big dinner together the day we all came back, and we talked for such a long time! It was great.

Claire (I'm going to use our English names so I can practice them) got a boyfriend over the summer, and we are all so jealous, but we are also excited for her. I guess we won't see her as much on the weekends, because she will be going out to see him. They are from the same hometown, but he goes to another college, and since we can't leave our campus during the week, she can only see him on the weekend.

Tomorrow is my first class with my new foreign teacher. I'm so sad we don't get to have Samantha again. We had so much fun in her class, and she was really nice. Our new teacher's name is Anne. I think it's a little easier to say (but I also think that my English is better than before). I asked Samantha if she knows her, and Samantha said they just met. I think it will be great, except this class is reading instead of speaking. It seems like we might not have a speaking teacher this year.

September 7th

Wow, Anne's class is so hard. She didn't smile as much as Samantha does, and she uses a lot of big words. Some of them I couldn't understand, and she talks fast, so I didn't have time to look them up in the dictionary.

At the beginning of the class, she told us she had talked to Samantha about us. Of course, I want to know what Samantha said. I really, really hope it was good things. Anne only told us that Samantha said we worked hard, and she thought we have a lot of potential. (I had to ask Anne about that word after class.) I wanted to know so much what Samantha thinks of us, so I tried really hard to write down the sounds, but I also ended up missing the next several sentences Anne said. I hope it wasn't too important. Anne explained that *potential* means that we have the ability to do lots of great things. I still didn't understand, so she had to explain it again and change some of the words, but I finally got it. Her pronunciation is really hard to understand! But I also remember how hard it was to understand Samantha at the beginning. I think it will get easier with Anne too. At least, I hope it does. As my Chinese teacher taught us last semester, "No pain, no gains."

We didn't play any games today, and Anne had us use our books, even on the first day of class. Most of the students didn't have books yet, because they didn't know which book to bring. I had checked the schedule, so I had my book, and I had to share with the people next to me. It was complicated and took a while for everyone to find someone with a book who would share with them. Then we were supposed to read an article about windmills. It was not very interesting, and there were a lot of words I didn't know. I'm glad I had my book though, so

I could write the translations for the new words. After we read the passage, we had to answer some questions. I got all of them wrong except for one! It was terrible! I felt so ashamed. Anne also seemed disappointed that most of us couldn't answer the questions correctly. I feel like I'm letting Samantha down. I thought my English was so much better, but I can't even answer these questions!

After class, I heard several of the boys saying they were probably going to skip the next class. It's too hard for them. Not me. I never skip class. I am going to learn this. Remember, Becky, "No pains, no gains."

~Becky

November 29th

We had Anne's class today. I'm almost ready to give up. It's still so hard. The passage today was about a weird fish I'd never heard of before. There are still so many new words. I feel like no matter how many new words I learn, I never learn enough. I'm trying; I really am, but it just doesn't seem possible.

Today, there were only four students in class. I think Anne was mad, so I tried really hard to read the passage and understand, but I just couldn't do it. I think Anne was trying to be nice to us, but I'm having such a hard time understanding what she says. I miss Samantha. I miss our spoken English class.

I'm not even sure how I'm going to use these English words. I wanted to take the IELTS exam so maybe one day I can study abroad, but I don't think I will ever learn enough words to be able to pass it. Maybe I should just do business here in China, but then what's the point of learning all these English words? Is it even worth it to keep trying?

~Becky

December 3rd

I saw Samantha yesterday, and we decided to eat lunch together. I used to eat with her sometimes, but since she's not my teacher anymore, it's harder to see her and make plans. When she saw me, she said, "Hi, Becky!" and I was so happy she remembered my name! I was able to talk to her about so many things, and now I remember how much I love learning English.

She told me this class is more difficult than her spoken English one. Anne told her about how hard the book is, and when I showed the book to Samantha, she agreed that it was difficult. She flipped open the book to a passage about climate change and read it for a moment. Then she pointed to the word, *geoengineering*. "Do you know what this word means?" she asked. I looked at the Chinese definition I had scribbled in the margin last week. "Yeah, it's talking about a big way to solve the problem of global warming." She said, "Wow, I don't even know what that means. I don't think I've ever even heard that word before!" That made me feel so much better!

I told Samantha about my motto "No pain, no gains," but then Samantha said I'm not even saying it right. It should be "No pain, no gain." I laughed for a long time. I will have to remember the correct way to say that.

Samantha also said Anne is really happy to have me in class every week. That made me feel good. Sometimes I also want to skip the class like most of my classmates, but if it makes Anne happy to have me there, I can keep going. And now Samantha and I are going to have lunch again tomorrow so I can keep practicing my spoken English! We also talked about my other classes and some things about America. I love learning about America, and I really hope I can go there one day!

Ok, I am going to go study now! I am going to remember those words Anne gave us for homework, so I will be able to understand the next passage. I can do this! No pain, no gain!

~Becky

Boys Will Be Boys
Guoliang

Inspiration Words: Green and Skip

Guoliang (gwoh lee-ahng) opened his door as carefully as possible; then he crept down the hallway so he could hear his dad and grandpa talking in the living room. He didn't think about what would happen if one of them walked toward the kitchen for some water and happened to glance at him in the hallway. All he knew was that he had to hear this conversation.

His hand was still aching where he had received the stitches, but that was nothing compared to the way his father had shouted at him.

"What do you think you were doing, skipping classes and climbing over the school wall, Liu Guoliang (lee-oo gwoh lee-ahng)?" At this point, Guoliang knew his father was really angry. His father raised his hand, and Guoliang was afraid his father would hit him, but instead, he just ran a hand through his graying hair and sighed. "Let me guess, you were going to play video games?"

Guoliang didn't answer, but his father knew he had guessed correctly.

"Don't you EVER think about doing that again. Go to your room."

Guoliang sneaked a glance at his grandpa, but the stern expression he saw did little to comfort him. Usually his grandpa took his side, but he didn't see any help this time. Guoliang put his head down and went to his room. He took off his green shirt that was now covered in blood where he had wrapped it around his hand as he ran to the hospital.

Right now, Guoliang had to know if his grandpa was as upset with him as his dad was. What would they talk about? He had to know.

"Xiao Liang (ssee-ow lee-ahng) reminds me of you, you know," his grandpa was saying. He used Guoliang's nickname, which seemed promising.

"Why, because I was stupid enough to climb a wall and get my hand skewered by a metal spike?" His dad laughed sarcastically, and Guoliang felt his hope of being quickly forgiven disappearing.

How did I get my hand stuck on a spike? That was pretty stupid. Guoliang stuffed his hand into his pocket so he wouldn't have to see the stitches, but the ache was still there.

"No, but you did your share of running away from school. You should just be glad the walls didn't have spikes on them, or you would probably have ended up in the hospital, just like Xiao Liang."

Guoliang's father grunted, but didn't respond.

"I remember one time you ran away to the liquor store so you could have rice wine."

"Wait, how did you know about that?"

Guoliang wondered if he could peek around the corner of the wall and look at them. He wanted to see his father's face right now so badly. *I can't believe Dad ran away from school too!*

"Your teachers told me, of course. But I didn't punish you at home because running away and getting caught is part of growing up. I told them to tell me if you did it again, but when you didn't, I figured you had learned your lesson."

"Ha, that was my first drink of alcohol, even though it was just rice wine. My friends and I thought we were so cool—until we got back and saw the teachers waiting for us outside our dorm room."

"And Xiao Liang wasn't even trying to go drinking; he just went out to play some computer games."

"Yeah, maybe you're right. Maybe I was too hard on him."
"I'm just saying that he's a boy. And he's smaller than you when you ran away from school."

"You're right," his dad sighed again. "I'll go get him, and we can have dinner together."

Guoliang hurried back to his room and just closed the door and hurried to his bed before he heard a soft knock. His dad came in and stood in the doorway.

"It's time for dinner, let's eat."

"Ok." Guoliang stood up and squeezed past his dad, who ruffled his hair as he went by.

A New Path

Tan Shuwen

Inspiration Words: Notion and Reach

The family stood again, and Tan Shuwen (tahn shoo wuhn) smiled at the other members of her family. This time it was her father giving the toast. Shuwen knew he was proud of her and her score on the *gaokao* (gow kow—the Chinese college entrance exam after high school). She had worked hard every night and had come out ahead of most of her classmates. Her high score ensured that she would be able to have her choice of colleges to attend in the fall.

Shuwen rarely drank wine, but her parents had poured her a small glass and smiled at her, "You're an adult now. Enjoy yourself tonight," they had said.

Now her father was in the middle of praising her yet again. "My daughter, Shuwen, has showed her ability as a member of the Tan family. I'm proud to call her my daughter, and I look forward to seeing what she will add to the family business."

Everyone clinked their wine glasses, making sure to tap glasses with Shuwen, who sat at the place of honor at the round table, the seat facing the door. After she had taken a sip of wine and most of her aunts, uncles, and cousins had sat back down, Shuwen cleared her throat.

"Thank you so much for coming. I'm thankful for all of your support this year as I have prepared for and taken the *gaokao*. I'm so happy it's over—" Everyone laughed, and her younger cousin even gave her a high five. Everyone around the table understood the stress of the exam. "—and I'd also like to share my future study plan." Shuwen glanced nervously at her father. He was smiling at her, encouraging her to go on. "I actually plan to study medicine." Applause died before it had begun as her family members' hands froze in the air. Smiles froze on faces before turning into confusion, but no one spoke.

Shuwen had expected this response, but for some reason, it still seemed to freeze her thoughts. She knew her family expected her to study business so she could join the family business. Becoming a doctor was probably the last thing they expected of her. Unlike in other countries, doctors in China didn't usually get paid a high salary. They worked long hours, and due to outdated assumptions, sometimes didn't get a lot of respect. Once, as a child, she went to the hospital and had fallen asleep in her father's arms as they waited to see a doctor. She had jerked awake when she heard a patient screaming at a doctor about something Shuwen hadn't understood. When they finally did see the doctor, she remembered thinking that the doctor had looked as tired as she was—and she was a sick patient. But that meant society needed more doctors, right? She wanted to help people, and becoming a doctor would be a good way to help not just patients, but other doctors as well.

Shuwen tried to continue, but the awkward silence was overwhelming. Everything else she had planned to say had completely left her mind. *Don't look at Mom and Dad*, she thought. But she could see everyone else looking in their direction, and her eyes followed theirs until she saw her father staring back at her in disbelief and disappointment. So much disappointment.

No one clinked her glass and wished her good luck in her future studies, and Shuwen sat down a couple of moments later. She had said it. She looked back at her bowl of rice and noticed a piece of duck that someone had placed there. She picked it up with her chopsticks, but didn't eat it. She stared at her bowl and knew everyone was looking from her to her father and back.

The meal didn't last too much longer, and soon Shuwen and her parents were on their way home. All of them looked out the windows of the car, watching the city lights flash by. If the driver noticed their silence, he didn't mention anything.

Once inside their apartment, Shuwen swapped her shoes for the comfy house slippers and headed toward her bedroom.

"Shuwen," her father stopped her. "Your mom and I want to talk to you in the living room."

"Ok," she changed directions and sat down on the overstuffed couch that did not offer the comfort of sinking with her weight. Her mom sat down beside her, and her dad stood in front of a chair, but didn't sit down.

The TV was off, and the room was strangely quiet.

"Why don't you want to study business? The company needs someone with you and your skills. You would add a lot. You can choose which department you want to work in. Your mom could help you a lot if you wanted to go into the accounting side of things, and our marketing and sales departments also have great leaders. I even have hopes that one day you will be able to take over as president. But medicine? What do you plan to do with that?"

"I'm hoping to be a doctor."

"A doctor?" Both of her parents looked at her like she had lost her mind.

"How do you expect to support yourself on a doctor's salary?" Her father looked around him at the large, opulent apartment. "And where did you get all these strange notions? A doctor will have to study for a long time. Once you finally graduate, then you'll work long hours with little pay and struggle to earn respect."

"My math and science scores are higher than all of my classmates, and I really love those subjects. I also really want to understand disease and look for new ways to help people. And I want to try something different." Her planned speech had returned to her, and Shuwen said the words quickly before her parents could interrupt her or stop her from speaking.

She didn't need to worry because her parents seemed incapable of speaking after she finished. Judging by the looks on their faces, their shock didn't allow them to form words.

"I'm sorry to disappoint you, but I don't like studying business. I want to make new goals and see if I can reach them."

Shuwen's mom and dad looked at each other for several moments. Finally, her dad turned to her and said, "We'll talk about this more later. You can go to your room now."

As Shuwen sat in her room, wondering what her parents would decide, she turned on some music and finally relaxed. Her parents couldn't really stop her from pursuing her goals, although she did hope that they would let her pursue those goals in peace, rather than fighting her every step of the way. But whatever happened, Shuwen finally had confidence that she had chosen a path, and it was going to be the best path for her.

Journey of a Mooncake

Mooncake

Inspiration Words: Fortnight and Contemplate

I have been made for a high and noble purpose. I am one of the special foods in China, and I have the wonderful task of bringing joy to many people during the Mid-Autumn Festival as they enjoy eating me and admiring the beauty of the moon on this special holiday. I have been told that the night of the Mid-Autumn Festival is full of joy as the family gathers to look at the moon and spend time together.

This year, the holiday is on September 21st, but it's still near the beginning of September now. I have a fortnight before the holiday, and I can hardly hold back my excitement. At the factory, I was carefully prepared in two parts. On the inside, I am full of mung bean paste with a salted egg yolk in the middle. I've heard that this is the choice flavor for many Chinese people. Some of my friends contain nuts or dried fruit. Red bean and sesame are also common fillings, and sometimes I hear about taro or sweet potato. On the outside, I have a dense, breadish covering with my name stamped into the cake-like outer layer: Mung bean and egg (lv dou dan huang, loo-we doh dahn hwoo-ahng).

After I had finished baking, I was placed into a package; then put into an ornately decorated box. It's quite comfortable inside, although it's a little dark. There are four of us in here; two egg yolk flavors, and two lotus paste flavors. Since we can't see outside anymore, we aren't sure exactly what's going on, but we are waiting quietly for us to be delivered to the happy family who will eat us.

After several days, we are finally on our way! I think we are going to a company, and from there, we will find our way into the hands of a family. Once we arrive at the company, I hear someone talking, and I realize I have been given to an employee! He walks with me for just a short while before everything goes still again. I think we are still in the building, but it's hard to be sure.

The employee goes home (I can hear him turning off his computer and putting some things in a bag), but he doesn't take us with him. The next morning, he comes in and opens the box, and I finally get a look at his face. He's young and looks like he just woke up. His hair is carefully gelled, but his eyes are barely open as he studies us. Sadly, he then closes the box without moving any of us. I really thought he was going to eat us for breakfast, but I'm kind of glad he changed his mind. I want to wait and celebrate the festival with the rest of the family!

For the rest of the week, no one moves us, and I begin to wonder if the man is ever going to take us home. Perhaps he forgot about us. This time alone gives me lots of time to contemplate my purpose. Just as the family gathers to look at the moon, they also gather around mooncakes—a perfect representation of the moon's shape. As they marvel at the beauty of the moon, they also marvel at the delicious taste of mooncakes.

One day, as everyone is packing up, I realize the holiday has arrived! *Please pick up the bag and take us home to your family, young man!*

When the man picks us up and begins to carry us out, I'm so excited! Where exactly will we go? We leave the building and start walking outside. For the first time, I realize how wonderful that office was. It's so hot in this box, I feel like I am going to start melting—and I didn't even know I could melt. I'm pretty sure the sun is pointing directly at me.

Finally, we start moving down, and the air becomes more bearable. I realize we are in the subway station. There are lots of noises. I can hear the beeping as the doors open and close; several people nearby are talking and laughing, and someone is playing phone games—sounds like guns shooting, but it's hard to tell for sure. After one of the beeps of the door opening, I suddenly feel pushed. The box is sturdy, and I'm thankful because I can feel the sides starting to close in on me. This subway must be very crowded. I hope it's over soon, before the beautiful stamp is destroyed!

We are finally off the subway, and the man is swinging us back and forth. He's also whistling, and I think he's excited for the holiday. I am too. Soon we will meet his family.

When we arrive at the young man's house, we are placed in a corner and we can hear the happy chatter of the family, but we can't see anything yet. Finally, after waiting for such a long time, they open the box and take me out. I'm so happy they chose me first!

A woman, who looks like the young man, but older, takes me out of the plastic bag and puts me on a plate.

"This looks delicious! I hope everyone has enough room for a mooncake!" She calls to the other people in the living room.

The other people look too full to be able to eat any mooncakes, but I do hope they try. The woman cuts me into several pieces for everyone to share, and finally I am living my dream.

Through Your Eyes

Anne and Johnson

Inspiration Words: Pumpkin and Scream

Anne sipped her pumpkin spice latte and glanced at Johnson, who sat at the table across from her. Then she noticed a couple with a small child walk up to the Starbucks counter. Anne watched them gaze into the pastry display before they moved on to the drink menu that hung behind the counter.

Even though it was the beginning of October, Anne didn't feel the fall chill in the air (unless the air conditioning was on full blast), but she was still excited when Johnson suggested coming to Starbucks so he could buy her favorite drink for her. They usually split the price of meals and other activities, so Anne enjoyed the extra treat when he bought her something special. She was looking forward to quality time with him and getting to know him a little better, since they still had only been dating for a few months. Aside from the explosion of fall in her mouth every time she took a drink, however, and the air conditioning that kept her comfortable, the date already felt like a disaster. Johnson wasn't in the mood to talk, and Anne was wishing she had brought a book to read instead. Wasn't that the purpose of a date—to chat and spend time together? She wasn't sure how she was supposed to get to know someone on a deeper level when that someone wasn't talkative.

As the date lengthened, and the couple she was watching left after enjoying their drinks, Anne started to fidget. Johnson still didn't meet her gaze, and she wondered if she should just go home. It was still raining outside, and Anne's shorts were still damp from her bike ride over here. Even though she had a raincoat and wore tall rubber boots, she couldn't hide from the ceaseless drizzle that had covered the roads. A truck had driven past her, right through a puddle, splashing muddy water across her legs and shorts. She had wanted to scream in frustration—some people didn't think about how their actions affected anyone except for themselves.

"How's your drink?" She asked as Johnson sipped his latte.

"It's good."

"Good!" Anne looked back toward the window. The rain dripped down from the closed umbrellas in the umbrella stand near the door, forming little pools of water. Delivery guys came and went, dripping in their full-body rain suits. Anne certainly didn't envy them their job.

When Anne felt like she couldn't sit still any longer and had grown tired of tipping her cup back to try to get the last few drops of the delicious liquid, she suggested they go on a walk around the mall.

"Sure," Johnson replied.

They stood and headed toward the entrance that led to the mall, away from the drippy weather outside.

Is this guy even going to speak to me today? Anne started to wonder as they walked along in silence.

"How was work this week? Anything crazy happen?" Anne tried to make some light conversation.

"It was normal, nothing unusual."

Exasperated, Anne looked at her watch. "Do you just wanna head back home?"

"Sure, if you want to."

"Well, I want to talk to you, but that doesn't seem like an option today." Anne tried to keep the bitterness out of her voice, but she didn't succeed.

"Oh, I was just enjoying the environment."

Anne nearly made a biting comment about the environment being strained, but she remembered back to the earliest days of their dating relationship. They'd had a lot of fights about their different expectations, and Anne had finally started to realize that sometimes it was enough just to enjoy his presence.

"Ok, maybe after we walk around for a while, we can talk some before we go?"

"Sure, that sounds like a good idea."

After they had wandered through several stores, Johnson asked her about her plans for class the next week, and Anne smiled as she talked about some games she planned to play with her students.

An hour or so later, Anne gave Johnson a hug and hopped on her bike. The miserable drizzle had stopped, and even though the trees still dripped, she was thrilled she would be able to go home without wearing her heavy raincoat.

****

Johnson stretched his legs out as he sat at a table in Starbucks. He knew Anne liked Starbucks, and she said last week that she had been missing her hometown and the cooler weather that came with autumn. Since his job required him to welcome foreign businessmen when they visited China, he knew foreigners seemed to like the seasonal coffees Starbucks offered. Maybe Anne would feel less homesick if he treated her to one of their autumn drinks, even though he thought they were a little strange.

Anne hadn't arrived yet, but Johnson didn't mind. Now he had time to scroll through the news from today and see what was going on in the world. Anne preferred that he put his phone away during their time together, and he tried to comply.

Coronavirus updates.

Typhoon in the Northern Indian Ocean.

Fuel Shortages in Haiti.

Looked like some tough stuff going on in the world.

The door dinged, and Johnson looked up to see Anne coming inside. He slipped his phone into his pocket and gave Anne a half-hug when she came up to him. She seemed a little damp.

"Is it still raining outside?" he asked, as they walked to the counter

"Yep," Anne continued talking about how a crazy truck driver had splashed dirty street water all over her.

"That's annoying," Johnson said, glancing back at her splattered clothes. "What do you want to drink?"

When they ordered their drinks, Johnson flashed the QR code so the worker could scan it for payment. He liked buying things for his girlfriend, even though they usually split the cost of things. It made him feel good.

Johnson watched as they mixed the drinks and put a thick layer of something creamy and white on top. "What's that white stuff?" he asked Anne, pointing to the drinks as the worker put the lid on them.

"Oh, that's whipped cream," Anne answered.

They took the drinks back to a table in the corner. Johnson was curious about this drink. He had ordered the same as Anne because he figured she probably understood the Starbucks menu better than he did. She had said it was a pumpkin coffee. He didn't usually drink coffee, but hopefully this one was good.

Tentatively, he took a sip. It was different than he expected. Having pumpkin in a drink seemed strange. He'd only had pumpkin as a dish at dinner, rather than a flavoring for drinks. He took another sip and tried not to make a face. It was super sweet. *They should market this as a dessert, not coffee,* he thought.

As Johnson nursed his coffee, his thoughts drifted back to the news articles. He wondered if the fuel shortage in Haiti would influence the fuel market in other countries. He didn't have a car, but several of his friends had cars, and they were always talking about how expensive gas was. Would this make it even worse?

"How's your drink?" Anne asked Johnson.

He tried to bring his thoughts back from world news to his girl-friend, who was looking at him and smiling. He stared at the funny concoction in front of him. It wasn't bad. It was a little weird, but it was pretty good. He decided to go for the simple answer. "It's good."

There was also that coronavirus update. He wondered what the situation in America was like right now. He thought about asking Anne, but she seemed distracted by something outside the window. He made a note to read the article later.

He glanced toward Anne. She really was so pretty. For such a long time, he had thought her long eyelashes were fake. And he was still amazed at her gray eyes. Pretty much everyone he knew had brown eyes, or sometimes, eyes so dark they could be black. But hers were gray. They were special.

When Anne suggested they go for a walk in the mall, Johnson agreed and was glad when she took his hand, lacing her smaller fingers between his. He walked along, glad to be inside out of the muggy autumn weather and to just be with his girlfriend. Anne asked about work, and he gave his usual answer. He tried not to think about work after he left the office, and he didn't think Anne would understand if he did try to explain it.

"Do you wanna just head back home?"

Johnson was surprised she was ready to go already. He felt like they had just arrived, but if that's what she wanted, then it was fine with him. She seemed irritated by his answer, but he wasn't sure why.

"I was just enjoying the environment," he said, using his other hand to motion to the shops around them.

Anne didn't answer right away, and Johnson was wondering if he was upset when Anne suggested they talk a little more later. Johnson remembered that she liked when he asked her questions. He tried to think back over the last hour or so and couldn't remember if he had asked her anything yet. What could he ask about? She had asked him about his work; maybe she wanted to talk about her classes. She did seem to enjoy talking about her classes and her students.

"What are you gonna do in your classes this week?"

Anne smiled and launched into a discussion of her plans. Johnson smiled too. He was pretty sure he had nailed it. When she hugged him before they left, he knew he had been right. For some reason, she really liked it when he asked her those simple questions. He should try to remember that from now on.

Broken Mosaic

Tan Shuwen

Inspiration Words: Butterfly and Card

Tan Shuwen (tahn shoo wuhn) lay on her bed. It was late Tuesday morning, but she hadn't left her bed since Sunday night. *That horrible night.* Against her will, her thoughts returned to those moments at the restaurant. She tried to think of something else, but she couldn't manage to pull her thoughts away from the things he had said to her.

She opened her phone and swiped through some of the recommended videos on her TikTok For You page, but she didn't see anything that could distract her. She didn't laugh at the video of a man trying to take money from his wife's purse while she slept. She swiped to the next video of a dog running aimlessly around a park. The screen of her phone was shattered. Last night it fell off her bed, and the screen was now a broken mosaic of whatever she was trying to watch.

"Wen Wen (wuhn wuhn), here's your lunch," Shuwen's roommate announced gently as she and the other roommates entered quietly.

Shuwen had given her roommate her campus card to pay for lunch, but now that she was back with food, Shuwen had no desire to eat. "Just put it on my desk."

"Come on, you really should eat it. If you wait, it will be cold and nasty." Another roommate came over to stand near Shuwen's bed.

"I'm not hungry."

"We got your favorite soup dumplings!"

"Thanks, just leave it there. I'll eat it later."

"Our anatomy teacher asked about you today. We said you aren't feeling well."

Shuwen didn't answer.

"Do you wanna talk about it?"

"No."

Shuwen wished her roommates would go away. They were being so considerate, and it made her feel worse. She knew she couldn't stay in bed forever, but maybe if she just stayed here a little longer, the ache would go away. Maybe she would stop feeling his arms around her when he hugged her, and maybe she would stop seeing his kind brown eyes burning with anger like the last time she saw him.

Sometimes, in the last few days, she had thought of his anger, and sometimes that helped. *How can I be with someone who is so angry? And the things he said! I don't think he ever loved me!* But then she would remember the week before, when he bought her flowers and chocolate just because, and told her how much he loved her. She tried to push away the dichotomy. Her head ached, and she knew she should eat.

"We're gonna go to the library. Send us a message if you need anything, okay?"

Shuwen knew she needed to go to the library also. Midterm exams were coming soon, and their classes this semester were hard. There were so many things to memorize, but right now, she couldn't make herself care.

"Ok." The door closed behind them, but she could hear them chatting out in the hallway. They were probably talking about her, but again, Shuwen couldn't make herself care. She knew they wanted to help, but she didn't know how to help herself, so how could she let her roommates help her?

Maybe I should eat some food. I guess it might help my headache. She left her phone on her bed, face down so she didn't have to look at the shattered screen. It reminded her of her shattered heart. *Everything in my life is broken.*

She nibbled at the food, but quickly gave up and went back to bed. As she lay there, she wished she could stop looking at her phone, but the impulse was so strong, and she couldn't think about anything else. *Maybe he texted me. Maybe Mom texted me again.* The only ache that matched the ache of missing him was the one that came when she thought about her conversation with her mom on Saturday. *Why did I tell her about him? We were fine before she found out.*

Shuwen again heard the accusation in her mom's voice, *If you really want to be a doctor, don't you need to focus on your schoolwork, rather than wasting time with a guy?* Shuwen knew her parents were still disappointed in her for choosing medicine over business. And maybe she had made a stupid choice. She couldn't please her parents; she couldn't please her boyfriend, and now she was going to fail her classes because she couldn't even study.

Thinking wasn't helping Shuwen to feel better, so she tried to watch her favorite TV show. A few minutes later she gave up, because it was too hard to see what was going on through the cracks on her phone. She lay on the bed, both wishing again that he would text her and also somehow dreading seeing his name on the screen. *He won't text me. He can't. Why does it hurt so much to end it? Why do I feel so broken? Will I ever be whole again? Why was he so mad that I hadn't told my parents? We've only been together for a year. My friends have kept their relationships a secret for a lot longer, and that never bothered their boyfriends. It's not that strange. Besides, I was doing him a favor—my parents probably wouldn't have been happy that he was dating me, would they?* The questions felt endless.

Shuwen drifted into a light sleep, dreaming of that Sunday night once again. Maybe if she had just done something a little differently, there would be a new outcome. Maybe if she had introduced the topic in a funny way, he would have laughed instead of exploded. Maybe if she had agreed with him and said she should have told her parents earlier, their relationship would have been okay. But when she woke up, she realized that nothing had changed except the position of the sun.

Shuwen sat up. Her head was still pounding, and she knew she had to get up. If she didn't die from a broken heart, this lifestyle would surely kill her. But at the thought of moving, she fell back against her pillow. Her phone vibrated against her arm, and she reached for it, her heart racing. *Mom.*

"Hello?" She hesitated as she answered.

"Hi, did you already have dinner?"

"Not yet."

"It's pretty late. You should go eat."

Shuwen tried to hold back, but just hearing her mom's voice deepened the ache in her heart. "Mom, we broke up on Sunday. He was angry that I hadn't told you about him. He thinks I'm ashamed of him. He said it's impossible to have a real, successful relationship if no one knows about it."

Shuwen waited for a response, but her mom was quiet.

She took the silence as encouragement and poured out the whole story. By the time she was finished, she was sobbing.

"I just made some of your favorite steamed bread. I'll send you a package; it should arrive in a few hours."

Shuwen sniffled, and a small piece of her heart felt better. Growing up, her mom always made her steamed bread when she was sad.

A few minutes later, Shuwen left her dorm room to go find her roommates and join them for dinner. She kept her broken phone in her pocket as she looked at the bushes and trees lining the sidewalk. A butterfly fluttered around some flowers, and Shuwen realized that not everything was broken, and not everything that was broken would remain broken forever.

Pressing on to a Better Life

Street Cleaner

Inspiration Words: Hand and Consider

Twice, he pushed the pink broom methodically away from him before pausing to sweep the leaves and other debris into the wide dustpan. He didn't glance up at the cars passing him or the bikes that swerved around him.

Brush. Brush. Collect.

Brush. Brush. Collect.

The rhythmic motions allowed his mind to drift while his feet and arms did the work. His wife told him to be careful and watch out for crazy drivers, but watching every bike or car that drove by was too exhausting. Most of the time, he just relied on the neon yellow stripes on his blue uniform to warn people he was there.

Most of the time, he didn't think about anything, but today, he was considering his daughter. While he was here on the street, she was in a classroom, in university. She was graduating in June, and he was so proud of her. He had never told her that, but everyone could see it when he smiled at her. She would be the first one in the family to finish university.

He got to the end of the curb and paused under a tree to wipe the sweat off of his forehead. It was nearly November, and after a breath of fall, summer weather was back here in Southern China. Even this early in the morning, he was hot. His pointed straw hat kept some of the sun off his face, but he could still feel the powerful rays through his blue uniform. He took the thick, white gloves off his hands. They protected his brown skin from the sun, but they were also so hot. He stood in the shade for a moment, looking at people heading off to work.

Right now, his daughter would be in her marketing class. When she was younger, he would ask her questions about her classes, but in the past few years, he contented himself with learning just the names of her courses.

He had been looking forward to her graduation and seeing her get her first job. He had been completely baffled last night when she called and told him and his wife that she wanted to continue studying to get a master's degree.

"Haven't you been studying long enough? Aren't you ready to get a job?" He had asked.

"I've been trying to get an internship, but I'm having a hard time finding something good. My grades are pretty good, but this school also isn't very famous. You know bosses are always looking for people from well-known universities. I've been trying to take a lot of tests so I can get certificates, but I just don't have enough time to study for all them. Since I don't have enough certificates, the better companies don't really want to hire me. It's hard to compete with people who've graduated from better universities."

He had looked at his wife helplessly. Who wouldn't want to hire her? She obviously works hard!

"I think if I get a master's degree, I'll be able to find a better job."

"You know that we'll support whatever you decide to do," his wife spoke, and he nodded, forgetting that his daughter couldn't see him over the phone. "If you want to get a master's degree, we also want you to do that."

"Thanks, Mom and Dad. I really have been working hard, but it's just hard to find a job."

He and his wife agreed. They wanted their daughter to be able to work in the field that she had studied and prepared for. And since neither of them had been to college, maybe they should trust that she knew what was necessary in today's job market. He certainly wanted more for his daughter than to be a street sweeper.

He kept walking along the street.

Brush. Brush. Collect.

When his dustpan was full of leaves and dust, he dumped it into a trash can on the sidewalk. He knew his daughter would never give up. He often felt like he hadn't taught her much, but he had taught her to persevere. Keep studying hard. Keep working hard. Keep collecting certificates at university. Keep collecting trash on the highway. Sometimes that's all you could do.

Blank Slate

Wang Mingge

Inspiration Words: Bottle and Disappear

Wang Mingge (wahng meeng guh) stared at the piece of chalk in her hand that was poised over the blackboard. She knew her students were watching her, and her heart pounded. *How do you spell* hierarchy? *Is it purely phonetic or is it more like the word* higher? After another moment of agonized thought, she wrote, "higherarchy" on the board and then turned back to her students.

A hand shot up from Lily on the front row. "Shouldn't that be spelled h-i-e-r?"

"Oh yes, of course, how silly of me." Wang Mingge forced a laugh as she corrected the word on the board. "Let's talk about what a hierarchy might look like in different situations." She sipped tea from her water bottle, hoping that would hide her burning cheeks. *What is wrong with me lately? I have a master's degree in English translation, and I spent three years in New Zealand. I've only been back home for a year—is it normal to be forgetting words already?*

At the end of class, Wang Mingge told the students their homework, and the moment the bell rang, the students began gathering up their books and packing their bags. Lily came up to the podium to talk to her, and Wang Mingge smiled, "Thanks for catching my mistake with *hierarchy* earlier."

"No problem. Teacher, I wanted to talk to you about our homework."

"Yes, did you have a question about something?"

"No, I just wanted to ask if we could have a little less homework this week. We have a speech competition coming up and several of us need to prepare." When some of the other students heard Lily mention the speech competition and homework, they hung back rather than rushing out the door.

"Yes, Teacher, we really have a lot of homework this week, and we are afraid we won't be able to complete it all," another student chimed in.

Wang Mingge suppressed a sigh and smiled again. *Why does our department allow the students to bargain about their homework? I try to be reasonable. . . .* "What would you like to change?"

Lily placed her notebook with the carefully-recorded homework on the lectern. "You asked us to read at least three news articles, but I really think it's more practical to only read one or two. That way, we can focus on reading that article well, rather than spending all of our time looking for other articles."

"Okay, that's reasonable."

"Thank you, Teacher!" The students hurried out of the room, smiling and waving.

Wang Mingge closed her books and turned off the computer. But instead of picking up her bag and walking to lunch, she sat down and put her head in her hands, letting her long black hair fall around her hands as she leaned over. *Mondays. Ugh.* She was relieved the long morning of classes was over, but she still had a lot to do this afternoon to finish getting ready for the week. And it was going to be a long week. She needed to finish working on that research proposal because it was due soon. And she needed to study English for herself. *I've been back for a year. Why am I still struggling to get back into the swing of things? And why do I keep forgetting simple words?*

Last week, Wang Mingge had said *permanent* instead of *temporary*, and the students had been really confused when she tried to explain that the agreement was "only a permanent solution." Today, she forgot how to spell *hierarchy*. *What am I going to forget next? If I keep forgetting these things, how am I going to be able to keep my job? Are the students going to report that I keep forgetting words? What if they give me a bad review?*

Wang Mingge thought back to her time in New Zealand when she could focus on learning rather than teaching. She missed the time when she could just focus on writing papers and hanging out with native English speakers. She missed her friends there, and she also missed the relaxed lifestyle. *I wish I could go back.*

"Long day?" Wang Mingge looked up to see her friend and colleague, TingTing (Teeng Teeng), standing in the door and smiling with sympathy.

"Yes! And it's only Monday!" Wang Mingge groaned and grabbed her bag so she could walk to lunch with her friend. "How were your classes this morning?"

"Oh, you know, the usual."

The elevator doors opened, and Wang Mingge was grateful it was empty. The students cleared out of the top floor pretty quickly because they knew they would have to hurry if they wanted to get their lunch without having to wait forever.

"I'm pretty sure my English is disappearing. I've only been back in China for a year, and already I'm forgetting words and I can't spell correctly when I write a word on the board."

Tingting laughed, "That happens to all of us. I even talked to Richard, and he said he even forgets how to spell words sometimes—and he's from England! It must be something about how a chalkboard magically wipes your memory."

Wang Mingge finally smiled, "He really said that?"

"Of course he did; don't worry so much. Read more news articles."

When Wang Mingge laughed, this time, it was genuine. "Now I

feel like your student," she said.

"It really works! That's why we tell our students to do it."

"You're right, as always."

The elevator dinged, and the women got on, leaving the classrooms behind them for the time being.

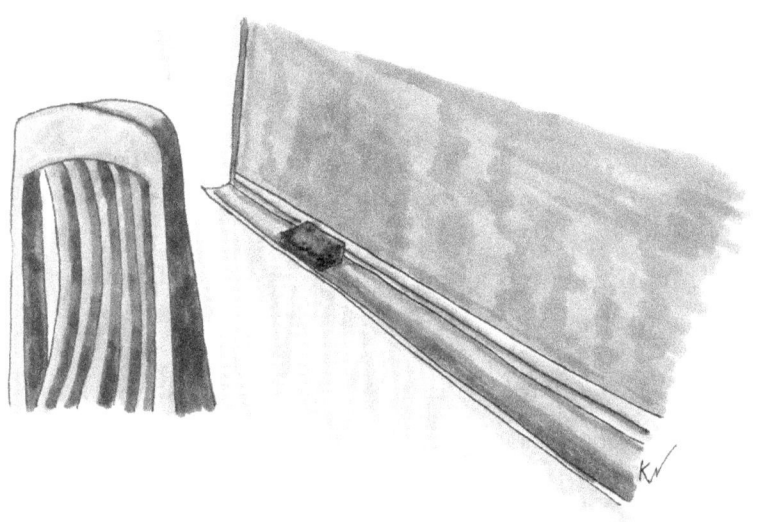

Just Keep Singing

Anne and Johnson

Inspiration Words: Shimmer and Bonus

"Let's go to KTV! My family is going next week, and they invited us to join them." Johnson and Anne sat sharing a bowl of *Ma La Xiang Guo* (mah lah sseeahng gwoh), a dish of meat and vegetables that had been stir fried together.

Anne stopped eating and started laughing until she looked at Johnson and realized he was serious. "Wait, you actually want to go?"

"Yeah, why not? Don't you like to sing?"

Anne's laughter started to turn into panic, and she felt her heart constricting. "Umm . . . "

"We're going to take you to KTV!" It was Anne's first year in China, and she loved hanging out with her students. She was willing to try anything. Last week, they had taken electric bikes to the beach for a Chinese-style barbeque. The week before, it was a traditional opera downtown. Anne's students were excited to introduce their country and culture to her, and Anne was excited to learn.

Anne agreed to go before she even asked what KTV was. In fact, the most information she got about it was that it had something to do with singing.

"You like singing, right?" Her students asked.

"Sure, singing is great!"

Friday night, Anne and her students met at a KTV just outside campus. Even though it was still early evening, music blared from several of the rooms they passed. The hallways were dark, and for the first time, Anne started to wonder what she had agreed to. Sure, singing was great, but they would be singing together, right—not like a performance or anything?

The worker showed them into a room, turned on a disco light and promised to return soon with the drinks. Drinks? This is a drinking thing? Anne didn't really enjoy drinking, and the thought of being the only sober person in a group of drunk students sounded less than appealing.

"You can sit here on the couch!" Jane, one of her students, shouted over the music that was already playing. "We're going to choose some songs! What do you want to sing?"

"Oh, um—" Before Anne could decide, Jane joined her classmates at the side of the room where a computer screen allowed them to see the available songs and choose ones they liked. Someone put on a Jay Chou (choh) song, and one of the guys grabbed a microphone that sat on the table. It was covered in glitter and shimmered in the light.

Anne admired his voice, but nobody else seemed to be paying attention. Everyone was still gathered around the computer adding songs to a playlist.

"What do you want to sing?" Jimmy shouted over to Anne.

"Umm, what are my choices?" Anne joined them at the computer, looking over their shoulders as they searched for and added their favorite songs to the line-up.

"Let Anne choose a song, everyone!" Jimmy made room at the computer and went back to the main page. "Which singer do you like? Maroon 5? Adele? Taylor Swift?"

"Ummm," Anne rarely listened to pop music and wasn't sure she could even name a song from one of those singers. "Do they have any Disney songs?"

"What kind of songs?" Jimmy shouted over the music as it built into a crescendo all around them.

"DISNEY!" Anne shouted back.

"DO YOU KNOW THE SINGER?"

Anne searched her brain. Who sang those songs anyway? "No! I only know the name of the songs!"

"WHO?"

"CAN YOU SEARCH THE SONG?"

"OH! OK!" Jimmy clicked around until he found another search page. "WHAT SONG?"

"Ummm . . . A WHOLE NEW WORLD?" Anne had no idea if she could even sing that song, but it was worth a shot.

"NOT HERE!"

Anne wracked her brain for another choice. "How about CAN YOU FEEL THE LOVE TONIGHT?" Surely, they would have The Lion King. Everyone loves The Lion King.

Jimmy typed the words into the computer, and a couple of songs popped up. Anne chose one she hoped was the right version and headed back to her seat.

For the next several hours, Anne kept waiting for the song she chose to come up, but it never seemed to come. Her students sang song after song. A couple were in English, but most of them were in Chinese. She was surprised by the beauty of some of her students' voices and cringed at some of the others. But even though she enjoyed listening to many of them sing, the songs started to blend together since she couldn't understand any of the Chinese songs.

The students passed drinks around, but she declined. It was beer, and she didn't care for the taste. Unfortunately, the quality of singing deteriorated as the level of intoxication went up.

Anne had just decided her song would never come up when Jane sat down next to her. "WHAT IS YOUR SONG?" She shouted.

"CAN YOU FEEL THE LOVE TONIGHT," she shouted back.

Jane went back to the computer, and as soon as Angel finished the Cantonese song she had been singing, Anne's song came on, and Angel handed her the mic. The intro was soft, and the students got quiet. Anne actually felt like she could finally breathe a little.

The lights still danced around them, but Anne closed her eyes, waiting for the dots to signal that it was time for the first words. She managed to get through the song, and the students all cheered. She knew she wasn't a great singer, and she didn't enjoy singing in front of others, but by now, her students were so drunk that no one really cared.

"WHAT TIME ARE WE GOING HOME?" she shouted at Jimmy during the next song.

"WE DON'T HAVE TO LEAVE UNTIL 2 A.M.! WHEN WE TOLD THEM YOU ARE OUR FOREIGN TEACHER AND WE WANTED TO SHOW YOU CHINESE CULTURE, THEY SAID WE COULD HAVE A BONUS TWO HOURS! ISN'T THAT GREAT?"

Anne leaned against the back of the couch and glanced at her watch when Jimmy picked up a spare microphone to join in the song that was currently blaring from the speakers. It's 10 p.m. now, so that's four more hours. I can't do this. Anne asked Jane where the bathroom was, and she left the stuffy room. As soon as the door was closed, Anne felt immediately better. She hid in the bathroom until she felt like she could face the noise again.

By 11:30, Anne was fighting to keep her eyes open. "I'M SORRY, JANE, BUT I NEED TO GO HOME. YOU CAN KEEP SINGING WITHOUT ME."

"BUT THERE ARE STILL SOME SONGS WE WANT YOU TO HEAR! AND YOU ONLY SANG ONE. YOU SHOULD SING ANOTHER ONE!"

Jane begged and cajoled until Anne agreed to sing one more. Anne had to wait another hour for them to put her song at the front of the long playlist, and by the time it was her turn, she was struggling to find her voice and remember the tune. She finished, apologized to her students for leaving early, declined the pleas to stay, and went outside with Jane, who led her back to the entrance. The night air and peace from the empty streets calmed her as she walked back to her apartment.

Anne tried to take a deep breath and push the memory away. She looked at Johnson. *I may as well be honest.* "Sorry, I really don't like KTV—too many bad experiences I guess."

"Oh, ok." Johnson looked disappointed, and Anne felt terrible.

"Maybe we can try it sometime with just the two of us instead of going with your whole family. I think if I could have at least one ood experience, maybe I wouldn't feel so stressed just thinking about it."

"Ok, good idea. We can do that instead!" Johnson smiled and gave nne a piece of chicken that he found in the depths of their shared bowl.

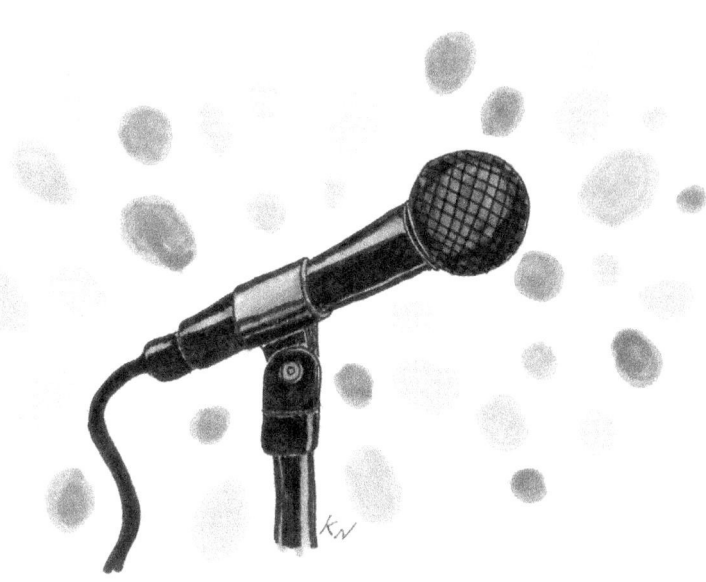

Desperate Prayers
Ellie and Carina

Inspiration Words: Red and Well

"I'm just so lonely, Grandma." Ellie tried to find a comfortable position on the hard, wooden sofa with her feet propped up on the coffee table. She balanced her phone between her knees so her arms wouldn't get tired holding it and turned up the volume for the video call.

Grandma smiled at her across the miles. "That's normal, honey. How often do you see that American family?"

"I only get to see them on the weekends because they are really busy with their kids and homeschooling and everything. They suggested I invite my students to lunch and ask them to show me around the city. I tried to invite some of them to lunch, but most of them are really nervous. I think they're afraid of me."

"I think they're probably more worried about their own English ability than anything else."

"Yeah! Almost every conversation I have starts with, 'I'm sorry my English is so poor . . .' Yesterday, I told my students that it's okay if their English is poor; I still want to talk with them, but I'm not sure how many of them understood."

"Just think about how you felt when you went to Mexico with your

Spanish class in high school. You struggled to talk to the locals down there, even though you had been studying for a few years."

"Yeah, that's true. I just wish I had some friends to talk to. I've been here for a month, and I haven't even been to see the Terracotta Soldiers yet!" Ellie glanced at the clock. "Oh no, Grandma, I just saw the time. I have to go to class; I have one at 10:10." Ellie's free period on Tuesdays was in the morning, and she was glad she didn't have office hours with her university teaching job, so she could easily talk to her family and friends back home. But she always hated saying goodbye.

"Ok, have a great day!"

"Thanks, bye!"

After class, Ellie headed to the cafeteria by herself. Her students smiled at her, but they were still a little hesitant to talk to her—especially in this class, so she hadn't even tried to invite anyone to lunch.

At the cafeteria, she ordered some noodles—consulting a notebook (where she kept notes about Chinese words or foods she wanted to remember) so she could get some that were not too spicy. On her way to her usual corner table near the window, she grabbed chopsticks and a spoon, balancing them carefully on the rim of her bowl.

At the table, she began the complicated process of using two sticks to transfer slippery noodles from her bowl into her mouth. The process was messy and a little humiliating. *I should have ordered rice*, Ellie thought as another noodle slipped from her chopsticks back into the bowl. But she hadn't ordered rice because she didn't know how to order from the rice restaurants. She came here because her American friends had taught her the name of this dish, and it just seemed the safest.

Halfway through the meal, she started crying. She convinced herself it was because the noodles were so spicy, but she knew the shop owner only put a little of the red powder on top of the noodles. Seeing the groups of friends around her, Ellie wished she also had someone to talk to. As she ate, she tried to pray, but it took so much concentration to eat the noodles, she had a hard time focusing. Most of her prayers started with, "God, please provide a friend I can talk to. . ." and ended with ". . . please help me to get these noodles into my mouth."

Her stomach was still growling after twenty minutes, and her bowl was still mostly full. *One day, I will conquer this. Who knew that noodles could be your archnemesis?* she thought.

"Excuse me, is anyone sitting here?"

Ellie's head shot up in surprise, and another noodle slipped back into her bowl. "No, please join me." She smiled at the petite girl who slid onto the bench across from her. "My name's Ellie."

"It's nice to meet you, my name is Carina."

"Wow, that's a beautiful name!"

"Thanks, I chose it because I wanted something special and different."

"Your English is great! What's your major?" When the girl paused, Ellie hurried to explain the word *major*, "What do you study?"

"Ahh, I study business, but I also learn English so I can do international trade."

Ellie almost forgot about her noodles as she talked with Carina about her major and her classes.

"Where are you from?" Carina asked while Ellie began another battle with a clump of noodles.

"I'm from the United States. What about you?"

"I'm a native of Xi'an (ssee-ahn)."

"That's so cool! I can't wait to go visit the Terracotta Warriors."

Carina paused in confusion, and Ellie jumped in with one of the only Chinese words her grandma had taught her, "In Chinese, they're called the *Bing Ma Yong* (beeng mah yohng)!"

"Ahh, yes! Well, actually, I've never been to see them either."

"What?" Ellie looked at her in astonishment. "But they're so famous, and they're right here in this city!"

"Yes, I guess I just never got around to it. They're always there, so always meant to go, but I never have."

"What if we go together? I've been so excited to see them, but I heard they are far away, and I don't know how to get there. Don't you have to take several different buses to get there?"

"That's a great idea! I think there are a couple of buses; I can check the route. How about this weekend?"

"Definitely!" Ellie set aside her chopsticks and pulled out her phone. Can I have your WeChat, and we can talk about the plan more later?"

Ellie walked back to her apartment with a full heart, although her stomach was still a bit empty. Her dream of seeing those Terracotta Warriors was coming true, and even better than that, she had made a friend.

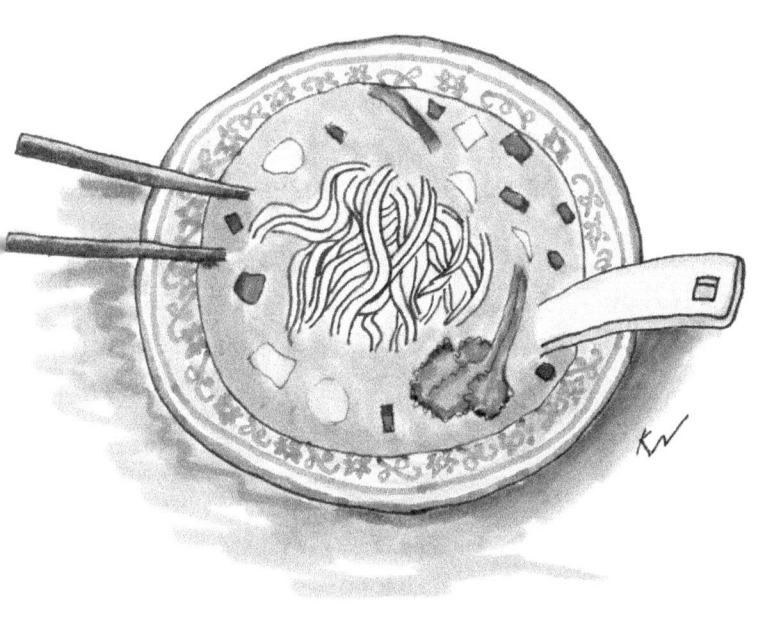

Numb the Ache
College Student

Inspiration Words: Mercy and Bond

I ended the call with my mom and climbed into my bed. I'd been trying to call her more frequently, after what happened. Inside the mosquito net, I felt like maybe I could hide from my roommates. It was the middle of the day, but since it was a Saturday, having one or more of us taking a nap in our beds was not unusual.

My three roommates kept playing their computer game and didn't seem to notice that I hadn't joined in again. I put in my headphones and turned the music up, hoping the strong beat would drown the shooting from the game and numb the ache growing inside of me.

All of my first memories are with my grandma. She cooked for me, played with me, and took me shopping with her. She scolded me when I was bad—which was often, and she told me I would be fine when I cried.

In primary school, I took the bus to school every morning and home every evening. One evening, I wasn't paying attention and I got on the wrong bus. When I realized it was the wrong bus, I didn't know what to do. I stayed on until the bus stopped, and the bus driver asked me where I lived. After I told him, he told me to wait for him on the bench at the bus stop. I sat and waited, wishing Grandma were there. She would know what to do.

When the bus driver came back, he had a motorcycle and he told me to get on the back. I obeyed, and he drove me home. The wind was strong, but I held on to the back of the motorcycle just like my dad had taught me when he took me on his motorcycle for the first time two years before.

When we arrived at my house, Grandma was standing in the doorway. She asked the bus driver what happened, and he explained that I got on the wrong bus. Grandma looked at me for a moment before wrapping her arms around me, "Next time, be more careful about which bus you take." Her voice was stern, but she hugged me tightly, and I was glad Grandma was always here to watch out for me.

Since Grandma was a Christian, she often told me stories about Jesus and the great things He did on Earth and the mercy He offered to people. When I was young, everything made sense. But then I went to school and realized that the stories Grandma told me were just nice stories. No man could really do those things Grandma told me about.

In middle school, my parents sent me to boarding school, and I only got to see Grandma on the weekends. They said it would be good for me, because I would learn independence and I would be able to focus on my schoolwork. I didn't tell anyone, but I was mad at my parents. I wanted to keep living with Grandma. She understood me, and she cooked me the food I liked—her spicy duck was the best. When I went home, she always cooked my favorite dishes. No matter what happened at school—if my friends were mean to me or if I'd done badly on a test, I knew I could always count on a big hug the second I walked in the door on Friday nights. She would reprimand me for making a mess as I devoured her duck wings and would throw a napkin at me as I wiped my dirty fingers on my shirt. She rolled her eyes, but sometimes I saw a glimpse of a smile before she turned away.

High school meant another boarding school, but since this one was farther away, I could only see Grandma once a month. Still, every time I went home, she made my favorite steamed buns and spicy duck.

Now that I'm in university, I haven't seen Grandma for more than a month. My parents pushed me to go to this university that's bigger and farther away from home. By this point, I knew better than to disagree, but I still miss Grandma. Our bond wasn't as strong as when I was little, but I know she loved me up to the end, and even though I never told her, I also loved her.

I tried not to think about the spicy duck and Grandma's hugs, but it's hard not to think about something when you're trying so hard not to think about it. I wished I could cry, but I just let the pounding in my ears match the scream in my heart. Maybe I would feel better if I went outside. But I didn't move.

For the first time in years, I thought about Grandma's faith. She used to tell me that after she died, she was going to go to Heaven to be with Jesus. That was His mercy—if we believe that He died for our sins, we could be with Him in Heaven. If anyone deserves to be with Jesus, I believe with all my heart that Grandma deserves it. But she would have said no one deserves to be with Him. He is perfect, and we all do bad things. I wanted to ask about the bad things Grandma had done, but I didn't.

Is she with Jesus now? If she's with Him, can she still see me? Can she still cook spicy duck in Heaven? Does anyone there think it tastes as good as I know it is? Does Jesus eat spicy duck? Grandma said He wasn't Chinese, so maybe He wouldn't like Chinese food? I think He must like it. Everyone likes Grandma's spicy duck.

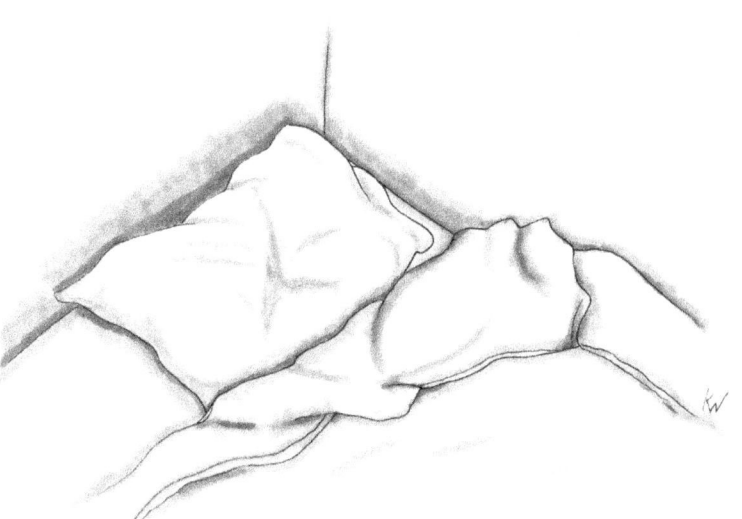

Where's the Path?

Paul

Inspiration Words: Bell and salary

Paul stared at the computer screen before leaning back and rubbing his eyes. It was 8 p.m., and the office was still full. Most people were sending emails, contacting customers in the West, and trying to hammer out the details of various business deals. A few people scrolled through their phones, hunched over take-out food in plastic containers on their desks.

I think I can be done in one more hour; then I can go home, and it will finally be the weekend! This month, for the first time in over a year, he could finally look forward to the weekend as his days off. This weekend he was planning to meet up with Cai Ling (tsie leeng) and his other friends, and he was so glad he had time to see them again. But he missed his job at the training center.

The email notification on his computer showed that his client had responded, and Paul found himself missing those dozens of WeChat messages from his students. Sure, he sometimes got annoyed, but at least at the previous job, he was interacting with people he had actually met. He'd gotten into the habit of writing mental "Pros and Cons" lists since he'd started this new job. At his old job, he worked a ton, but at least he had the mornings to relax, since they worked afternoons and evenings. He thought working a 9-6:30 job meant he could leave at 6:30, but that wasn't the case. Sure, now, he had Saturdays and Sundays off like his friends, but from Monday to Friday, he worked twelve-hour days. This job had no time for any kind of life except for what he could squeeze into the weekend. And the worst part is that the salary was lower.

Please confirm the price, and we will ship the goods to you on the date you requested. Paul typed the email and hit send. At least he still had the chance to use his English, but foreign trade wasn't something he was passionate about. And sending emails hardly counted as using English; he couldn't remember the last time he had spoken a word in English out loud. When the training center closed, Paul decided that maybe it was a sign to try something besides teaching. At that time, he was exhausted and he missed his friends.

But now he missed work that meant something. He missed interacting with real people—people that were more than just a name in the "To" or "From" slot in the email message. Not only did he lack a passion for foreign trade, but he was also still exhausted. And even on the weekends, he had to check his inbox and make sure he was on top of everything.

At 8:50 p.m., a distant bell rang in his mind. At the training center, a class would have been ending at this time. He looked around the office. Most of his colleagues had left, and Paul decided it was time he could also head home.

He turned off his computer, grabbed his bag, and nearly ran out the door. It was good to be on his feet again! Sitting down all day in cheap chairs sure didn't feel good for his back.

"Hey, Fu Hao (foo how)! Wait up!"

Paul turned, still surprised to hear his Chinese name after finally getting used to his English name. His co-worker was just coming out of the building and walking toward him.

"Oh, hi, Xin Kun (sseen koon), are you headed to the subway?" Paul said.

"Yep! Man, it sure is good to be out of the office!"

"Couldn't agree more," Paul and his colleague started walking. They had about ten minutes to walk, and Paul wasn't really feeling up to chitchat.

"I think I'm gonna quit," Xin Kun said, after a moment of silence.

"Really?" Paul looked at his co-worker in surprise. "But you've been here for even less time than I have. You only started two weeks ago!"

"Yeah, but this isn't what I signed up for at all. Didn't it say 9 a.m. to 6:30 p.m. on the job description? It's 9 p.m. now. And I have barely seen my girlfriend since I started. I think she's about ready to break up with me."

"That does sound complicated. What are you gonna do when you quit?"

Xin Kun laughed bleakly, "Look for another job—hopefully I'll be luckier next time."

"Hope so. Do you want to keep doing international trade?"

"I don't know. If I do, then I'll probably run into the same problem. All the communication has to happen at night, and that eliminates any kind of life."

"Yeah, that's true."

"But what else can I do with an English language degree?"

"I'm right there with you. I feel like there are fewer and fewer options these days."

Paul said goodbye at the subway as they headed toward trains going in opposite directions. *Why am I doing this job? Maybe I should quit like Xin Kun. I don't have a girlfriend telling me I should, but maybe this isn't the best choice. I don't have any sense of accomplishment when I go home. There's always another email to send or another customer to try to talk to. It's like an empty cycle of . . . nothing.* Paul leaned against the corner of the subway car. Even now, after 9 p.m. the seats were all taken.

But do I really wanna go back to the training center life? Do I really wanna go back to working until 11 p.m.? And giving up weekends? Paul popped his headphones in and allowed himself to stop thinking as the hip-hop beat sounded in his head.

Yes, if I'm going to spend so much of my time at work, I want to be doing something I enjoy. If I have to give up time with friends, I may as well give it up for something that means something. Maybe I can try a kindergarten instead of a training center.

Wedding Dresses and Eggs
Anne, Samantha, and Becky

Inspiration Words: Candy and Surreal

Anne looked around her at the hotel room in Hunan province. Samantha sat on a chair staring at the door where Becky had just walked out.

"Can you believe our little Becky is a bride?" Samantha said the words as if she was in shock.

"Definitely not. I will always see her as my little sophomore, the only one who came to that hideous reading class faithfully."

"I know! You know she was in the first class I ever taught? Walking into class, I was so nervous, and I remember she was sitting there in the first row with a pen and a notebook already on her desk, ready to learn.

"Students like her can change the whole feeling of a class. In that IELTS reading class, I felt like no matter how much I tried to help them, it was hopeless. I don't know what I would have done if Becky weren't in that class."

"Yeah, and I'm really glad we were able to start having weekly lunches with Becky. I feel like, after a few weeks, she became a friend, not just a student.

"Man, we would talk for hours! Those lunches gave me a whole new perspective of our students. They might struggle with class materials sometimes, but outside of class, they're so excited to communicate."

"Okay, but here's the big question," Anne paused and glanced toward the chair where Becky had been sitting. "Do you think she really loves this guy? I mean, everything happened so fast."

"I know what you mean; it makes me wonder if she is only doing this because her parents just really wanted her to get married."

"I know; she always hated going home for the holidays because her parents would ask if she had a boyfriend. She would always say she was just trying to focus on learning English, and a boyfriend could wait."

"Do you remember that one year she came back from the National Day holiday, and she said her mom had dragged her to a restaurant to have dinner with some guy who was the son of her mom's friend?"

"I will never forget that story! She felt so uncomfortable that she ran away to the bathroom and didn't come out for twenty minutes. When her mom went to check on her, she pretended to have diarrhea. So awkward."

"Becky is such a special girl. I really hope this is what she wants. And this guy had better be good to her!"

Anne checked the clock—11:45 p.m. "If we want to go see Becky in the morning, we really should go to sleep soon!"

"But we still have so many things to talk about! I want to hear all about Johnson!"

"I'm sure there will be time tomorrow! If I start talking about him now, we won't go to sleep for another two hours, at least!"

The next morning, Anne and Samantha hurried up to Becky's room, but by the time they got there, the room was already crowded with bridesmaids in matching dresses. When they arrived, someone let them in, and they saw Becky sitting on the bed with a bright red dress spread out all around her. A photographer squeezed between everyone, trying to take pictures, and Becky smiled at her previous foreign teachers while still posing for the pictures. Peacocks were sown into the top half of the dress, and a large strip of fabric lay across the bright red skirt with more peacocks. A golden headpiece circled around her black hair that was secured in a bun.

"Where is the guy?" Anne whispered as she gave Becky a quick hug.

"He's not here yet. He's supposed to come to the room and give us red packets, but don't let him in until he has given us lots of red packets with money inside!"

The doors closed, and everyone in the crowded hotel room became more excited as all the bridesmaids started talking.

"I think he's outside," Samantha said to Anne, trying to peer around

the wall that led to the doorway.

Red packets were passed around the room as the groom pleaded for entrance, but the bridesmaids refused. Only when had given several dozen red packets and sang a song and done some push-ups was he finally allowed to enter. Once inside, everyone made a place for him to kneel in front of Becky, who still sat on the bed, surrounded by her skirt. She smiled graciously the whole time as the photographer snapped dozens of pictures.

Anne and Samantha studied the groom. He was thin and not very tall, but Becky was shorter than he was. His black hair was slightly long and just disheveled enough to make them think he wanted it that way. His hands were shaking when he took her hands in his own.

"Make a speech!" Someone called out.

The groom tried to smile, but his lips shook, and Anne felt a little sorry for him. Finally, he began the speech.

"Becky," he looked into her eyes, "from the moment I saw you, I have loved you. I love meeting you on the way to work and walking to the subway with you every morning. I love that you always buy me a *baozi* (bow dze; steamed buns) and soy milk because you know that's what I love, and you know I wake up too late to have time to buy it for myself. I love spending lazy Saturdays with you in our favorite coffee shop, and I love watching TV shows with you for hours while we laugh together. There is no one in the world I would rather spend the rest of my life with than you."

Anne and Samantha could only understand snatches of the declaration, but Becky translated it for them later, and they all smiled at the adorable little speech. During the conversation, Anne focused on the groom's smile and trembling lips. He almost cried, and Anne could see that he meant the words.

Maybe she could trust this man with her dear friend. Becky was more than just a previous student. Becky was the person who had helped her to navigate the difficulties of first-year teaching. When she had been confused and frustrated, Becky had been there to translate things and offer advice. When she went to the office with her questions, and they told her to just ask the students for help with administrative things, Anne always went to Becky. And Becky had been there for her. Becky had been one of Anne's first students in China, but more importantly, Becky had been her first friend.

After the speech, everyone went to the cars that were lined up outside of the hotel. The groom took Becky on his back and carried her to the car, according to tradition. The cars snaked through the city, passing the old district of the city and the ancient city wall. Anne assumed they would end up at the restaurant for a big celebration meal, but instead, they first stopped at another hotel.

This room was full of balloons, and the bed was covered with a bright red comforter. Someone told the children in the room, presumably nieces and nephews, to look for the candy, and they soon found candy under the comforter, along with lots of dyed eggs.

Anne and Samantha stood off to the side, a little uncertain about what they should do. They smiled and took the candy the children offered them, feeling it was a little like Easter with candy and dyed eggs. Becky and her groom smiled for more pictures, and Anne smiled too as she watched them. Being here in a new place with such good friends from her first years in China felt a little surreal, and Anne still found it hard to grasp that her little Becky was getting married. But Anne could see that Becky was happy with this guy, and that was the most important thing.

They headed to the next hotel for the big dinner and celebration. They talked with Becky's friends and family, trying to understand the Chinese that was tinged with a local accent. They smiled at everyone, even when they didn't understand, and tried to look like they knew what they were doing (although they usually didn't). They didn't get much more time to spend with Becky, but as they saw the new couple raise their glasses for a toast, it was easy to see their love for each other.

Far from Home

Ellie and Qunying

Inspiration Words: Remorse and Plate

Ellie pulled another sweater over her head and put on her coat. Then, she wrapped a scarf around her neck and pulled a hat over her ears. She was nice and warm inside, but the moment she stepped out into the gray day outside, she knew the cold would seep through her clothes quickly.

Thanksgiving Day, and here I am going to class. Ellie heard an alarm on her phone go off, telling her it was time to leave as she shoved her feet into her boots. *At least I only have morning classes today, but still. It's a holiday.*

As she waited for the elevator, she felt her phone buzz. *Happy Thanksgiving, sweetheart.* Ellie's eyes started to fill with tears, but she brushed them away. She had cried enough already this morning, and she didn't really want the wind hitting wet cheeks.

Thanks Mom, she replied to the message.

Love you, and hope you have a good day today.

Ellie stuffed her phone in her teaching bag. It was better not to think about her family getting ready for Thanksgiving. Her grandparents and cousins were already in town. Grandma would be looking for someone to tell her stories to. Ellie's old room had been converted into a guestroom, and she knew everyone would be exchanging news from the past year and playing games all evening. Mom would put the turkey in the oven—

Ding! The elevator doors opened, and a blast of cold air hit her as she walked outside.

What am I doing here? In her heart, she knew she was exactly where God wanted her. She had become close friends with several of her students, and she was so happy to be able to love them and make a difference in their lives, but it was hard to remember all that God was doing when her heart missed home. *Is this worth it?* Remorse seeped into her heart as the cold air forced its way down her collar and up her coat sleeves.

Her phone buzzed again, but she didn't take her hands out of her pockets to check it until she got to class. When she did finally glance at the message, once again, her eyes filled with tears.

****

Qunying (choon yeeng) closed the oven door and adjusted the timer. Another thirty minutes before she'd have to add another layer of seasonings and butter to the turkey. She glanced at the clock. Already 3 p.m. Only three more hours before everyone would arrive. Before then, she still needed to do the potatoes, the salad, something about a green bean casserole—*Oh no… the bread!* Qunying lifted the towel where her bread was supposed to be rising. Good, she hadn't missed it.

First, I'll finish the bread. Qunying tried to hum, but her mind was too busy organizing everything she had to do to focus on a song. Maybe she could turn on some music. Nope, her hands were already dirty. And besides, there was no time. As she finished arranging the rolls on the baking pan, she realized she couldn't do the bread now because the turkey was still in the oven, and there wasn't room for anything else. *Oh well, the dough should be fine until the turkey finishes . . . I hope so at least. As long as the turkey is good, nothing else really matters, right?* She glanced into the oven at the turkey that had consumed every waking hour and several of her nightmares over the last several days. Last night, she had been ready to give up on that horrible bird, but she knew her American friends would love to have a turkey for their Thanksgiving celebration.

Qunying thought about their faces and their excitement when they would walk in the door. She had never cooked or even eaten turkey before, but the young teachers that came to her house for games and dinner once a week had mentioned how much they loved turkey on Thanksgiving, so Qunying had splurged (and it was a splurge!) to buy one for the occasion. This morning, one of them had said there was a new American teacher at her school, and Qunying had agreed to let them invite her also. It was going to be a full house.

A couple hours later, Qunying stooped over a bowl of potatoes and mashed them feverishly with a fork. *Only one more hour. I haven't even started the salad, and there's still that box of stuffing, but I think that should be fast.* Suddenly, Qunying nearly cried out at the sharp pain in her back. She paused for a moment with her hands on the table, unable to move. After a few moments, she stood slowly and tried to stretch the aching muscle.

"God, you know I'm trying to give a blessing to these American teachers and friends," Qunying prayed aloud, "but why did You allow this pain to come now? Can't You please make it go away?" She tried to do some slow stretches, and the pain slowly lessened. She needed to sit down and close her eyes, but there wasn't time.

She left the potatoes and started washing the lettuce for the salad. Qunying's husband came home, but she didn't notice until he put his hands on her shoulders.

"It smells wonderful in here!" He said and reached toward the turkey that sat on the counter.

"Thank you, can you help me? My back hurts, and I can't finish mashing those potatoes. Can you mash them with that fork?"

At 6:15, their guests began to arrive, and Qunying was relieved they were a little late. After directing her husband to put out the plates, Qunying slipped into a back room to put on a fresh shirt—one that wasn't stained with turkey grease and specks of mashed potatoes and milk.

When she returned to the kitchen and living room, Qunying had a smile for everyone and hugged the new friend named Ellie, who looked like she was about to cry. Qunying hoped the food would make her happier. *It must be hard to be away from family on a holiday*, she thought.

As everyone sat around the table, Qunying was thrilled that everyone was pleased with the food. She encouraged everyone to eat more, and they all did. They showered her with praises, and she thanked God for these friends and for the ability to bless them with food. She felt like her ministry of cooking and sharing food with friends was small, but hopefully she could encourage these people who were so far from home.

After dinner, they each shared what they were thankful for, and Qunying blushed when the first person thanked her for all the delicious food.

"I'm thankful that my students are still willing to work hard to study English—sometimes they're done with the semester by this time!" one of the Americans said.

"I'm thankful for some really good friends this semester, and I'm thankful that I don't have as many classes as I did last semester so I can see my friends a bit more," another teacher mentioned.

A quiet voice spoke up. "I'm thankful that you all invited me to come today. This is my first Thanksgiving away from my family, and I was really missing them when I got your invitation to come." Ellie's voice broke as she shared, and she looked down at her hands. A moment later she continued. "You have no idea how special this dinner has been, and I'm so thankful to be able to enjoy this time with other people who love this holiday. And of course, thank you, Qunying, for your generosity and your delicious food!"

Food is Life
Delivery Guy

Inspiration Words: Neon and Perhaps

Food. My life mostly consists of food. I'm around food all day, every day, but even though I'm around so much of it so often, I rarely have more than five minutes to eat a meal. Oh, and weather. The weather is also a huge part of my life.

Sometimes when I ask people to guess my job, they first guess I'm a chef or waiter when I talk about being around food so much. But as soon as I mention the weather, all my friends immediately know I'm a food delivery guy. Although now that I think about it, there aren't many people that fall into the category of "friends" these days. Working 9 a.m. to 9 p.m. every day doesn't leave much time for socializing.

Some of my fellow neon-yellow-shirted food delivery workers are friendly, but we don't usually talk much, except for a few shared words if we happen to be in an elevator together. I spend a lot of time in elevators, and I've gotten to know which apartment complexes have the fast ones and the slow ones. Although, I will take a slow elevator over eight flights of stairs any day. I dread orders to older apartment buildings because those high floors kill me when there's no elevator! Sometimes I joke that my job offers a free work-out program. Running from my electric bike to an apartment building and sometimes throwing in a few flights of stairs gives me enough exercise to sleep well at night.

The weather also makes a huge difference in how my day goes. While it's nice to have a sunny day, the heat can really sap my energy. And if it rains, I have to wade all over town in a heavy, full-body raincoat. Somehow, my clothes always end up wet too, which makes it even harder to run up those stairs quickly. But, hey, at least I get paid a little bit more on rainy days for the inconvenience.

When I first started delivering food, I used to get really hungry every time I entered a restaurant to pick up an order. In the winter, waiting for food to finish cooking at noodle shops was a special form of torture. Watching chefs stretch hand-pulled noodles, boil them, and then drop them into steaming bowls of soup before layering thinly-sliced beef on top always made my mouth water and my stomach rumble. By the time I could take a break for dinner, I would return to those shops because I had been dreaming about their food for so long. Even though it would be late, they would make up a bowl of noodles for me, and I would realize that restaurant workers also had a hard job. Not much of a break when there are always hungry customers like me who come in late.

Now, I hardly notice the smells when I enter the restaurants. I spend a lot of time on my phone while I wait for the orders to be ready, so I don't have to look at the other customers enjoying their dinners. In some cafeteria-style restaurants, the pre-prepared food sits in trays under heat lamps. People come in while I wait, pointing to the food they want, and the worker puts a small dish of vegetables or meat on a heaping bowl of rice. I try not to look at those dishes either—fried peppers and pork is one of my favorite meals. When I go to these restaurants late in the evening, there usually aren't many choices left, and what I get is usually only slightly warm.

Sometimes I wonder what it would be like to finish work at 6 p.m.

and go to dinner with the rest of the dinner crowd. I know I could choose different hours, but I get the most orders during dinner hours, so I try to always work during those times. And at least this job pays pretty well, so I'm not going to complain too much. It would be nice to have time for a girlfriend, though. Perhaps if I get a different job, I'll try to find a girlfriend. It would be nice to have someone to spend my free time with.

Another benefit of this job is that I don't have to think much—especially once I learned the area. I used to get lost in some of the bigger apartment complexes, but now I always know which building to go to, and I have even figured out which entrance is which. I am perfecting the art of shaving as much time as possible off of each delivery so I can make more deliveries and earn even more money.

Now that I'm more familiar with the area, I can let my mind drift to other things, like the business I want to start once I have enough money saved up. I have several good ideas, and I'm hoping I can get something to work.

One of my ideas is to have a video game café. Surely there can be a more interesting way to spend my evenings than playing video games at home. And I know people love milk tea and other drinks (I deliver dozens of those every day—especially to universities). So, I think I could open a café that gives people their favorite drinks and gives them something to do so they keep ordering more drinks! It's going to be great.

I heard that in my city, Shenzhen, they already have some cafés like this, and I've heard they're pretty successful. I just need to keep pushing through these long, monotonous days of picking up food, driving my electric bike, waiting in an elevator, driving, food, driving, food, driving, elevator, and more driving.

Find the Light
Zhanqi/Adam

Inspiration Words: Pilot and Light

Feng Zhanqi (fuhng jahn chee) stepped into the airplane hangar, savoring the last few seconds of bright sunlight. He walked toward the Boeing 747 and thought about how he would fix the problem in the small engine room. He would probably spend most of the day crammed into the small room with one of his colleagues, trying to find the problem and figuring out how to fix it. At the thought of the long hours in the darkness, he already missed the sunlight he had left behind him.

We'll probably be working on this airplane for the rest of the week at least. Zhanqi grabbed his tools and headed toward the plane.

Zhanqi had only graduated from college a couple of months ago, and he was still getting used to the rhythm of life in the hanger, fixing airplanes. He loved the work—he loved being around airplanes and making sure they were working properly so they could go where they needed to go, but he missed being in the sun.

Since he lived in Hainan, he still had time to go to the beach on the weekends. He would soak up as much sun as possible, saving it for the coming week when he'd be cloaked in darkness inside some obscure part of whatever plane they were checking or fixing.

After a full day of analyzing the problems in the confined area, Zhanqi headed home. To save money, he lived in a small dorm-style apartment near the hangar with three of his coworkers.

"Hey Zhanqi, do you want to go out for some barbeque with us tonight?" As he slipped off his shoes, his coworker and roommate grabbed his shoulder and tried to push him back out of the door.

"Come on, man, you know I have to study tonight." Zhanqi laughed and continued into the small apartment.

"But you study every night! It's time for a break."

"Not this time."

"But you don't take the test for four more months!"

"That's exactly why I need to study. I'm not gonna get my pilot's license by eating barbeque."

"I don't get why this is so important for you—we already have a great job."

"Of course, it's a great job, but can't you imagine how wonderful it would be to be flying those planes instead of fixing them?"

"Ok, fine, suit yourself."

After his roommate left, Zhanqi boiled a pot of water. He dropped in a few vegetables he had picked up on his way home, then some noodles, and finally, two eggs. He glanced at one of his books while he waited for everything to cook and continued reading while he slurped down the noodles.

He checked the time on his phone before washing the dishes. 7:30. If he could read this book for an hour and a half and the other one for another hour and a half, he could squeeze in a quick shower and still be in bed by 11:00.

Nearly every day for the next four months, Zhanqi followed this routine. Sometimes, he took a break from his noodles and books to eat dinner with his friends from university or get some exercise at the beach, but he stayed up an hour later on those nights to make sure he still got a few hours of studying in.

When the weekend for the test came, Zhanqi was less nervous than he expected. He headed downtown and arrived at the testing center thirty minutes before the test was supposed to start and confidently wrote his answers to almost all of the questions. The hours of studying had paid off, and he felt certain he would pass.

After the test, he went home. He would have to wait for a month before the results were released, and even though he was confident, he still had a small fear that maybe he had misread some of the questions or didn't know the information as well as he thought. The only thing to do was wait. And in the meantime, he needed to start preparing for the next exam, in case he passed this one. He expected the best and wanted to start preparing early for the next step.

When the results came back that he had not passed, Zhanqi was shocked. What had gone wrong? He had prepared so well, and he had been so confident on the test. Did he read the questions wrong or put them in the wrong section on the answer page? There was no way to find out. All that work; all those hours of studying, and he didn't pass. Zhangqi exited out of the website where the results were posted and stared blankly at the screen.

"Did you get your test results back yet?" His roommate asked.

"Yeah, I didn't pass."

"Really? Man, that's a bummer. I thought for sure you would have passed."

"Yeah, me too."

"Well, on the bright side, at least now you'll have time to hang out with us more."

"Actually, I'd better review all the material and try to figure out what I missed. I'm gonna take the exam again next year."

"But surely you can afford a short break. You have what, like, eleven months to prepare?"

"Yeah, I guess you're right. Maybe I could use a break."

"Glad to see you outside of the dorm room, Zhanqi!" His room-

nate said at the barbeque restaurant as they picked apart an eggplant
overed in minced garlic later that night.

"Enjoy it while it lasts! Soon I'll be back to those books. Next time
will definitely pass. But for now, at least we have jobs, right?"

Mr. Fisherman
Mikael

Inspiration Words: Fishing and Japan

Mikael (mee-kayl), a Russian student, labored through the Chinese
passage while his classmates listened to him read. When he came to
a word he couldn't recognize, he paused and waited for his teacher to
offer the word. He knew the second character was *yu* (yoo-wee), the
word for *fish*. But what was the character before it?

"*Diao yu* (dee-ao yoo-wee)," his teacher said.

"What does it mean?" Mikael asked, glancing up from his textbook
to look at the teacher who stood leaning over the podium with the
book open in front of her.

"Would you like the short answer or the long answer?" The teacher
took off her glasses and set them on the podium behind her, and Mikael
grinned sheepishly at his Japanese classmate next to him.

Sorry, he mouthed in Chinese. They both knew, along with everyone in the class, that they were going to get the long answer no matter
what they said.

While their teacher launched into the explanation of the impor-
tance of fishing for many Chinese people, Mikael's Japanese classmate
mimed the action of casting a fishing pole and reeling in a fish.

Mikael nodded and jotted the definition in his book. Then he focused his attention on the explanation his teacher was giving.

"*Diao yu* has many other meanings in the Chinese language. Has anyone played mahjong before?" Mikael looked around and noticed that only two students raised their hands, his Japanese classmate and another older European classmate who had lived in China for a long time. "Let me find a picture of the game for those of you who aren't familiar with it. I encourage you to learn how to play while you are here in China."

The teacher opened Baidu, the search engine that Mikael had quickly learned was the most common one in China, and located a picture of the board game. Blue and white tiles on a green carpeted board appeared. While the teacher continued talking, Mikael studied the shapes on the tiles. He recognized some of the traditional characters for the numbers on some of the tiles while others had various groupings of circles or sticks.

"This phrase can be used to describe someone who goes to a mahjong game with their friends, but doesn't take any money with them. Mahjong is usually played for money, but this person is apparently hoping to earn money before he has to pay, so you can say that this person is *diao yu*."

Mikael made another note in his book next to the phrase.

"But *diao yu* has yet another meaning. It can also be used to talk about a type of man." The teacher grinned, and Mikael and his classmates perked up. This could be interesting. "If a guy talks to a girl and shows an interest in her, but doesn't actually say he likes her, you can also use this phrase to describe him."

Mikael, who was short in stature but large in charm, leaned back in his seat and stretched his feet out in front of him. He felt something sharp between his shoulder blades and knew his fellow Russian friend was poking him. And even though Sofya didn't turn around from her seat on the front row, he knew she was thinking about him.

"Is it considered positive or negative to say that about a guy?" Mikael suddenly asked.

The teacher laughed and looked at him, "Of course it would be negative."

Oops, Mikael thought. He wondered if he should tell Sofya that he thought of her as more than a friend. Or did he? He still wasn't quite sure.

The teacher continued talking about other uses of *diao yu*, but Mikael had given up paying attention. He also didn't make any notes about the third usage.

After class, the students headed into the hallways for their twenty-minute break.

"Mr. Fisherman!"

Mikael looked up from where he stood next to the vending machine after the first class, trying to decide which drinks to get. "Oh, hey, man." Mikael gave his Ukrainian friend a quick handshake and shoulder bump.

"Watcha gonna get?"

"I think I'll just grab a couple of Cokes."

"A couple?" His Ukrainian friend raised an eyebrow.

"Yeah, I think my fishing days might be done."

The eyebrows went up even higher.

"Did you see where Sofya went?"

"Yeah, are you gonna ask her out?"

"I was thinking about it. Most likely. If you don't beat me to it."

The eyebrows fell, and he laughed. "Definitely not, man. I think she's sitting on a bench with one of her friends." He pointed in the direction of a few benches in a grassy area behind the building.

"Great. Hey, could you, umm . . . distract her friend for a few minutes?"

"Absolutely." While Mikael turned back to the vending machine, the Ukrainian headed off toward the two girls, most likely thinking of what he could say to lure away Sofya's friend.

Holding both ice-cold Cokes in hand, Mikael headed towards Sofya. *This is it*, he thought.

Where Family Comes Alive

College girl

Inspiration Words: Keep and Moon

I had begged Mom to let me stay home instead of going to Cong-hua (tsohng hwah), a suburb of my city, during the Spring Festival holiday. I know the whole family is supposed to get together for the most important holiday of the year, but sometimes I wish we could stay at home instead. Getting here was not bad, but I know that going home, the traffic will be horrible. Besides that, fifteen people crammed into a villa with nothing to do just didn't sound like that much fun. I think Mom was about to let me stay home, but then she mentioned that the villa has a KTV. She knows my weakness, and she knew I would come if there was a KTV. I wouldn't be surprised if she chose this villa just because she knew the KTV would convince me to come.

Now ten people are crowded into this large KTV style room, and I love the vibes. This is what Spring Festival should be like. The minute we arrived this afternoon, I headed straight towards the karaoke machine to see what songs they had, and I was impressed with their selection. They have enough to keep everyone happy. We could sing all night if we wanted to.

On the way here, my sister and I scrolled through TikTok videos on our phones, Mom napped in the front seat, and Dad stared at the road as he drove. A few minutes into the drive, he tried to roll down the window so he could smoke, but we complained because it was pretty chilly outside. Other than that, the only sounds were the clicks of my sister's and my fake fingernails on the screens of our phones. But here in the KTV room, it's like our family comes alive. My dad's second-oldest sister (we call her "Second Aunt" because of her order in the family) is here along with two uncles and all of their families. Grandma and Grandpa are coming with First Aunt tomorrow.

My sister and one other cousin are somewhere else in the villa, probably watching videos together, but pretty much everyone else is here in the KTV room.

We've already been here for an hour, and the song list is so long that adding songs now is pretty much hopeless. My younger cousin is in college now, and he is suddenly super interested in English songs. He's done two already. After the second one, he passed the mic along and plopped down on the couch beside me.

"What's with the sudden interest in English?" I asked.

"Oh, you know, it's just pretty fun to learn." He pulled out his phone like he was trying to ignore me, but I wasn't gonna stand for that.

"Ha, don't think you can fool me! There's probably a girl in your English class that you want to impress when you go back to school after the holiday, right?" I tried to grab his phone.

He didn't look up as he held the phone out of my reach. "I don't know what you're talking about, silly."

"Then let me see your messages. I bet you're getting ready to send her that video my dad took of you right now!"

He locked his phone with a click we didn't hear in the loud room and stuck it in his pocket. I felt like this action alone fully answered my question, and I smirked, "You can't keep secrets from me!"

Just then, my second aunt stood up as the familiar violin intro began to one of Teresa Teng's (tuhng) classics. We all stopped talking and watched. Teresa Teng was super famous in the 70s and 80s, but we all agreed that my second aunt's voice was better.

She stood in front of the TV with the microphone near her mouth, but she looked around at us when she started singing, "You ask me how deep my love is . . ." At least four of us pulled out our phones to take videos, and she smiled as she reached the most famous line, "The moon represents my heart (Yue Liang Dai Biao Wo De Xin, yoo-eh lee-ahng die bee-ow woh duh sseen)." We exploded into applause as the last note faded.

My second aunt loved singing this song, and we never got tired of hearing it. Of course, the song doesn't have anything to do with Spring Festival, but for me, each time I hear that song, I'm taken back to Spring Festivals in the past. I enjoy singing songs too, but this, right here—being with family and listening to my second aunt's beautiful voice— was the reason I loved KTV.

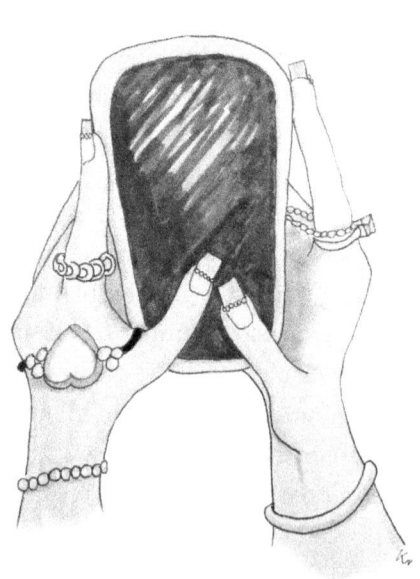

Stuck

Tan Shuwen

Inspiration Words: Italian and Cat

Shuwen (shoo wuhn) looked at her patient, who was waving her arms in circles and hitting anything they connected with. She tried to focus on calming her patient down, but Shuwen found herself wishing she could just swing her arms around in frustration too.

When Shuwen decided to devote her medical studies to brain research and helping people with severe mental disabilities, her friends all assured her she would be the perfect doctor. "You're so calm and chill; the patients won't have any choice but to calm down and listen to your advice." "If I needed help, I can't think of anyone I would rather have as my doctor than you." Her friends spoke nothing but praise of her choice and her passion. And Shuwen did love her work. She loved bringing peace to troubled hearts and minds. She loved finding beauty in people that society tended to ignore. But today, there was no peace in her own heart, and she didn't know how to give peace to someone else.

Shuwen and her colleagues had been locked inside the hospital for three weeks, and they had no idea when they would be able to leave. The number of Covid-19 cases in the city was nearing a hundred, and most of the cases had originated from an older woman who lived just down the street. Although everyone inside the hospital had tested negative, Shuwen hadn't left in the past three weeks. They couldn't have anything outside of the hospital delivered, and she was about to go crazy with the same hospital food and the same buildings around her all day and all night.

Half of her brain tried to think of ways to calm the woman in front of her and the other half thought about her cats in her apartment. *Are they doing okay?* Shuwen had asked her best friend to check in on them a few times and make sure they had enough food, but she was still worried about her dearest friends. The hospital consumed most of her time and energy, but going home to their welcoming, furry faces was the joy of her life. Shuwen had dated on and off in the few years she had been a doctor, but none of the relationships had panned out. Her cats were the one constant, and she missed them.

She missed the way she flopped down on the couch after taking off her shoes and immediately feeling Hei Hei (Hay hay, meaning *very black*) jump onto her stomach. Usually, the small, black cat would curl up and try to go to sleep while Shuwen rested after a long day. Sometimes he would push his nose into her hand, begging for attention. Coffee would rub against the couch and nudge her fingers if she left a hand hanging down for her. Da Vinci would observe the scene from his perch on the desk, unconcerned with whether or not he received any attention, but happy that she was finally there to give the other cats something to do instead of bothering him. She named Da Vinci after the Italian painter because she longed to go to Italy, but since she had no time for travel, she contented herself with the reminder of the wonderful painter in her house.

After resting for a few minutes, she would pop open the lid of the takeout that she usually picked up on her way home. Before her extended stay at work, the weather had started to get a little chilly, so she often picked up some noodles with soup. She would pour the lukewarm soup over the noodles and stirred them in, trying to separate the noodles that were starting to harden into an unbreakable mass. Hei Hei would jump onto the table and explore the lid she had set aside.

He was always exploring something, and he was the reason that Shuwen had to keep the trash cans covered. She had come home too many times to find the contents of the trash spread out across the room before she finally bought cans that you had to step on to open. Hei Hei wasn't quite dexterous enough for that yet, but she was just waiting for him to figure out how to get inside.

The woman suddenly stopped moving, and Shuwen's mind shot back to the present. The patient let out a low groan and clutched her stomach, a common gesture she used to show that she was feeling sick.

"I'm so sorry you don't feel well. I think it's time for you to get some rest." The appointment was over, and Shuwen walked out, wishing she could focus and think about how to help her patients today.

On her way to a quick lunch, she glanced at her phone. *I'm at your apartment, but Hei Hei's not here.* Shuwen heart stopped when she saw the message from her best friend.

What do you mean?

I left the window open the other day to get a little air in here, and I think Hei Hei must have gotten out onto your balcony and run away. I've looked all over the neighborhood, but I haven't seen him.

No. No. No. No. Shuwen wished she could hit undo on the text message and make it untrue.

I'm gonna check with some of your neighbors, but I just wanted to let you know. I'm sorry…

Shuwen headed to her temporary dorm instead of the cafeteria. There's no way she would be able to eat now. She wanted to puke. If anything had happened to Hei Hei, she would scream. She lay on her bed, wishing she could feel the small weight of her cat on her stomach. After 20 minutes, she boiled water for some instant noodles and stared at her phone while the noodles got cold.

Found him. Shuwen breathed again.

She was starting to answer the message with a joyful emoji, but another message came in first: *Your neighbor has him, and she won't give him to me.*

What?

Shuwen called her best friend, prepared for battle.

"Hi, Shuwen—"

"Let me talk to my neighbor."

"She won't talk to me anymore. I'm back in your apartment now because she barely even let me see him before she closed the door in my face. I think she's afraid Hei Hei will come out and go back to your place."

"Of course he will—because that's his home!"

"When I tried to get her to give him back, she said that she found him wandering around the halls crying. She saved him, and now she doesn't want to let him go."

"But that's my baby. She has to give him back." Shuwen felt her voice breaking.

"I know . . ."

"Did you offer her money?"

"Yeah, she refused."

"That cat is valuable. I paid several thousand yuan for him. She can't just take him, can she?"

"I don't know what else to try . . ." There was silence for several minutes while Shuwen tried not to cry, and her friend tried not to hear the tears in the silence. "At least he's safe for now. Maybe we can just leave him for now, and when you can leave, you can talk to her. Maybe she'll listen to you."

Two weeks later, Shuwen and her colleagues were cleared to leave. She didn't join them for the celebration dinner, but instead paid for a taxi to get home as soon as possible. The ride seemed endless. *What will I do if I can't get him back?*

When she knocked on her neighbor's door, she could hear Hei Hei mewing. He always did that when she had visitors also. Shuwen sometimes wondered if the little cat thought he was a guard dog. She didn't try to tell him no one was intimidated by his adorable little body, but she usually picked him up on the way to the door so he could see out while she talked to the visitor.

The door opened and her neighbor stood there.

Before either of them even said hello, Shuwen blurted out, "Please give me my cat."

"I found Xiao Hei (see-ow hay) without a home, and I saved him. He's my cat now."

"His name isn't Xiao Hei, it's Hei Hei. And I will give you anything you want. How much money do you want for him? Please give him back!"

"He's not for sale. He loves his home here with people who take care of him."

Shuwen tried to fight and tried to argue, but she finally realized it wouldn't do any good. "Can I see him?" She tried to peer around her neighbor who blocked most of the doorway.

"No. He's eating."

When the neighbor slammed the door, Shuwen stood frozen in shock, then turned around and opened her own door. She picked up Coffee and dropped onto the couch. Da Vinci turned to look at her and did something that he had never lowered himself to do when she came home from work. He stood, stretched, and dropped onto the floor. Then he walked calmly over to her, climbed onto her lap, and fell asleep as if this was his new spot.

In His Own World

Yao Bo

Inspiration Words: Running and Building

A small takeout container of rice and another small box with some chicken and vegetables sat on the table near Yao Bo's (yow bwoh) computer. He had started eating, but then he forgot about the food he had ordered when a zombie suddenly attacked him. Once he had killed the creature, he continued farming.

Most of Yao Bo's friends had stopped playing Minecraft and had moved on to other shooting games. He used headphones while playing now so he couldn't hear the gun shots and shouts from League of Legends, the newest hit game. Yao Bo knew he would never stop playing Minecraft, even if everyone else quit playing. Actually, he didn't care what they did. He was only mildly interested in what his roommates and classmates cared about.

His older cousin had first introduced him to the game when he was in middle school. At first, Yao Bo wasn't very interested in Minecraft. It looked fun, but he was too busy with other things to pay much attention to the game. Really, he was just too busy playing with his dog. Well, it wasn't actually his dog. He had found it one day when he was walking to school. He stopped to pet the dog, which was dirty and pretty pitiful. The next day, he had saved a piece of *you tiao* (yoh tee-aw; fried bread) from his breakfast and given it to the dog.

Soon, the dog was following him home and walking to school with him every day. As Yao Bo walked down the hill from home, the dog would meet him by the small convenience store where he bought a little bread. They would eat it together, walk down the street, up another side street, through some small alleys, and finally through the school gate.

Yao Bo didn't really care if the dog had a family, but he didn't seem to have anyone. Once school ended for the summer, Yao Bo and his dog would climb around the mountain park behind his house. Yao Bo tried to avoid other people, and his dog didn't seem interested in anyone besides his little boy. Fall came, and when Yao Bo returned to school, his dog waited for him at the gate every day.

During school, Yao Bo daydreamed about the dog, planning adventures for them to go on each afternoon. They would hike through the trees on the mountain or splash through the small stream, his dog faithfully following behind wherever he led.

But one day, the dog was gone. Yao Bo never found out exactly what happened to him, even though he searched everywhere. He would stay out each day, searching until the sun sank behind the mountain, and his parents grew worried about him staying out so late after sunset. He couldn't find the dog anywhere.

For weeks, Yao Bo walked aimlessly to school, stared out the window through class, wandered home, picked at his food for dinner, and went to bed. His teachers didn't seem to notice since he spent most of the class time staring out the window or doodling on some paper anyway, but Yao Bo felt the gaping hole in his life and his heart ached.

One day, when his cousin was visiting for a couple of days, Yao Bo again watched him playing Minecraft. The idea of building new things soon caught hold of his mind.

He started creating a world, and for the next ten years, he built and designed anything he wanted. Some of the people in his class liked to build things they heard about or saw in pictures or movies, but Yao Bo only enjoyed crafting completely new things. He loved the satisfaction of placing one block on top of another and creating something magnificent. He didn't usually talk much to his classmates, but he listened intently when they described their houses. He thought to himself that their constructions didn't sound very impressive—not compared to his.

Yao Bo spent every possible minute in front of the computer, building his houses, running from strange creatures, and discovering new places. He loved the limitlessness of the game. He explored the lakes; he built tall buildings into the sky. He built buildings made entirely of glass. Every time there were new upgrades, he saved up his money and bought them. His world was magnificent.

Once he had died from a sudden zombie attack, and he sat paralyzed. *Is everything gone?* His mind immediately remembered the emptiness he had felt when his dog disappeared. *This can't be happening again.* When he respawned, he opened up his virtual pocket. Everything was gone. After making sure his house was protected from the zombies, he went online to research a solution. *Okay, in the future, I'll store all my valuables safely in my house instead of carrying them around in my pockets.* He would make sure he would never lose the world he had created.

Yao Bo started shoveling rice into his mouth as he stared at the screen. *Maybe I should walk around and make sure everything is okay.* He moved the avatar around the screen, enjoying the beauty of the buildings he had created. Everything was perfect. The game was his home and his world. His animals were his friends, and he enjoyed walking around a world with no other people.

Yao Bo turned up the sound on his headphones once again to drown out the sound of shooting coming from his roommate's computer behind him. He climbed to the top of a mountain that lay roughly in the center of the world he had created. At the top, he turned his avatar to look at everything around him. He could see the magnificent boats on the ocean to the north. He could see his tree house village off to the east.

"Wow, looks like an impressive construction." Yao Bo turned to see his roommate staring at the screen.

"Oh, yeah." Yao Bo wished his roommate would go away. This was his world, and he didn't like to share it.

"Can I look around a little bit?"

"No. I have to do my homework now." Yao Bo exited the game and picked up a textbook.

"Ok." His roommate left and Yao Bo tried to study, but he was really thinking about what he was going to build next. Maybe he could make a new observatory.

When Will My Life Begin...

Ellie

Inspiration Words: Decide and Resentment

Ellie always sang while she got ready for class, and now she had music on almost constantly. Music felt like the only escape from this small apartment. It hadn't seemed so small when she moved in two years ago, but after spending the last seven days in lockdown, she had finally decided that it was small. She glanced out the window as her recent favorite song from the movie *Tangled* started playing: "Seven a.m., the usual morning line-up. . ."

She checked her watch and paused the music—time to join the online zoom class. She opened the zoom room and sent the password to her students. She greeted them as they joined the chat room, but once several students joined, they turned off their microphones and cameras, and she was left to just wait for the class to start.

She opened her textbook and tried to generate energy to share the lesson with her students while staring at random profile pictures. There were a few Chinese celebrities, cartoon characters, backs of heads, and occasionally, a Western face. Few students used their own faces in their profile pictures, so she only knew who they were by the English name next to the muted microphone icon.

"Today we're going to talk about shopping!" Ellie hoped her voice didn't sound as fake as it felt. For the fourth time that week, she plodded through the vocabulary and some warm-up questions, staring at those meaningless profile pictures that had become all she knew of her students. This class was particularly hard because she had never met these students, and she couldn't quite figure out how to teach them. *Are they too shy to answer the questions? Am I talking too fast? Do they all have a bad internet connection? Are they just lazy?* The questions played through her mind on repeat as she waited for someone to type an answer to her question into the group chat.

Thankfully I only have one class today. But this thought left Ellie feeling even more discouraged. She used to love class. Even before Covid-19, she had enjoyed going to class every day, but after a whole semester of online classes, she was thrilled to go back to regular classes. They were lucky enough to have had regular classes for a full year after the virus first arrived in 2020, but now there was another outbreak in her city, and they were in lockdown again. Ellie plodded through her days just trying to find things to do in the solitude of her apartment.

At 9:50 a.m., she wished her students a good day and closed the zoom room. Some classes told her thank you and sent her nice messages in the chat at the end of class, but today, only one student bothered to say anything. The rest signed out quickly, leaving Ellie to wonder what they had to do in their lives that was so pressing.

She hit play on the music, and as the familiar melody played again, she decided to join Rapunzel with the chores, sweeping her floor for the third time that week. She glanced at her bookshelf. She hadn't been back to America since she first arrived in Xi'an (ssee-ahn), and she had only brought a couple of books with her. Was it time to "reread the books" just as Rapunzel had done? She certainly had time to spare. Maybe she could call her parents or Grandma? Probably not, it was already getting pretty late over there.

Ellie climbed onto the window seat and stared out the window. And I'll keep wonderin' and wonderin' and wonderin' and wonderin' when will my life begin." Mandy Moore's voice merged with her own as she stared at the intersection down below. Almost no cars waited at the red light, and Ellie found herself missing the blaring horns that he had finally managed to tune out.

She stuck her head out the window and closed her eyes. She tried to pretend that she was on the top of a mountain, surrounded by grass and flowers and trees. She struggled to remember the smell of nature, and the feel of grass under her toes. That was one thing she had over Rapunzel—at least she knew what grass felt like, but that almost made the confinement more unbearable. She looked down to the bottom of the apartment building, all nineteen floors below her. She really was up in a tower.

She spotted a delivery man by his bright yellow uniform with the large yellow box on the back of his bike. *What should I cook for lunch today? Or should I order takeout? I'm sick of egg sandwiches, but everything else takes so much effort to make.*

Ellie scrolled through a few delivery options on her Mei Tuan (may twahn) app, but she still hadn't quite gotten the hang of the delivery system, and there still seemed too much Chinese for her comfort. Buying vegetables was a little bit easier. *But what to make?* Ellie didn't really enjoy cooking, not like her sister did, and even though she had learned a few dishes during the 2020 quarantine, she just didn't feel motivated to cook this week.

Ellie's gaze drifted back to the city outside her window. *This isn't what I signed up for.* Ellie tried to push it away, but she felt a tiny seed of resentment. The trouble was she wasn't even sure who she was mad at. She wanted to be mad at Covid-19, but that was just a virus. Was she mad at God? She didn't want that, but why didn't He take away this miserable virus? Was she mad at China? How could she be mad at a country for trying to protect its people, even if this lockdown did seem a bit extreme? She stared at a distant tree. *When will my life begin . . . again . . .*

The Trial
Ellie, Mikael, Adam

Inspiration Words: Gummy Bears and Floss

Ellie glanced around the darkened houses in the village. She had to act quickly, and her mission was urgent. Some dangerous characters lurked in this village, and she was outside after curfew, even though that was strictly against the village leader's orders. However, he had given her special permission to get some information tonight, and she only had a couple more minutes before time ran out.

The evening before, Ellie had arrived in the village and immediately knew something was wrong. But she'd only gotten a brief glimpse of the other villagers before curfew . As she glanced around at the houses, she finally made her choice and sneaked into the house of her friend, Adam. Her eyes darted around the room, searching for clues. First, she saw a bearskin rug in the living room, and she started to wonder if maybe he was a hunter. A mounted deer head on the wall seemed to confirm her suspicious, but she wanted to be sure. If Adam was a hunter, he could help her to find and eliminate the evil creatures in their village, but she had to be sure. If she trusted him and he turned out to be evil, she would be in serious danger.

She tiptoed into the hall and stopped. That was what she needed.

At the end of the hall, carefully mounted on a hook, was a bow and a quiver full of arrows. Adam was a friend who could be trusted. She picked up the bow, just to check that it wasn't fake, but she realized time was probably running out.

Ellie glanced at her watch. She had to go. She leaned the bow against the wall, forgetting to hang it up again. She ran back to her own house and closed the door just as another door at another house opened.

For the duration of the night, Ellie knew she was supposed to be sleeping, but instead she sat in a corner of her house and munched on gummy bears. She thought about the rest of the town and who could be evil. Every once in a while, she heard the howl of a wolf.

The next morning, Ellie slipped out of her house as soon as the morning bells announced that curfew was over. She first glanced at Adam. Would he know she had been in his house? She would have to reveal her information carefully if she wanted him to also trust her.

The neighbors peered around at everyone else as they slowly emmerged from their homes. Everyone here was either suspicious or guilty. She knew this. They had all heard the wolves last night. There had been rumors and reports of werewolves in the area, and the sounds last night convinced her that there were at least two werewolves in the village.

Which of her friends were guilty? She knew all of these people, but as she glanced around the circle in the living room of the Airbnb, she was unsure which of her friends she could trust. Adam, (his Chinese name was Zhanqi, jahn chee) was quiet and studious. He had just moved to the city after he got his pilot's license, so she didn't know him that well, but she was thankful she could trust him.

Ellie ran through the list of characters in her mind as well as their possible roles. If she could figure out who was good and who was a werewolf, she could win the game. She constructed a chart in her mind and looked around her. Who was playing the part of each character?

Role	Task	Who???
Seer	Can see one other character	Ellie!
Hunter	If voted out, can choose one other person. If he chooses a bad person, the good team wins, if he chooses a good person, the bad team wins	Adam

Troublemaker	Trades the cards of two other characters
Insomniac	Can see their own card at the end of the game
Robber	Takes another player's card and becomes that character
Drunk	Trades his card with one card in the middle, but doesn't look at it
Villager (2)	No special task—normal good person
Werewolf (2)	Bad character! If he is killed, the good people win
Minion	Bad character! If he is killed, the bad team wins
Tanner	Bad character (but on his own team)! If he is killed, only he wins

Mikael (mee-kayl), a Russian exchange student in Ellie's school, could never be trusted. His smile was too flippant, and he was so good at making everyone believe whatever he said. She glanced at him. He nodded at her, "Who are you, Ellie?"

"I'm a good person, of course, but I am less likely to believe the same of you," Ellie replied.

"Come on, what could I have possibly done last night? I was sleeping peacefully the entire night!" Mikael flashed his best smile, and Ellie rolled her eyes.

"I don't know who Mikael thinks he is, but I was also someone who was sleeping peacefully the whole night," Adam broke in. "But last night, someone was definitely in my house."

The bow. She'd forgotten to hang it back up. Ellie realized her mistake, but it didn't matter now. "I can vouch for Adam. He is a good character."

Adam looked at her. "Did you see who I am?"

"Yes, you're the hunter."

Adam smiled and nodded. "Ok, I can trust you too."

Mikael and the others watched the exchange. "Or, you two could
be werewolves." Mikael accused. "Or a minion and a werewolf."

"Come on, give it a rest," Adam said. "Who are you, anyway?
You're awfully suspicious."

"I'm just a villager." Mikael said. "A boring old villager."

Ellie wondered if perhaps she could trust Mikael today. *Maybe
he's actually good.*

"What makes you so sure someone was in your house last night?"
Sofya, Mikael's girlfriend, asked Adam.

"Something had been moved when I woke up. It wasn't where I
had put it when I went to sleep last night," Adam answered. "Do you
know anything about that?"

"As a matter of fact, I do." Everyone glanced at Sofya as she continued. "You are no longer the same person you used to be."

"What a troublemaker!" Mikael laughed as he pointed at Sofya.

"Sure, you could say that," Sofya smiled, and Ellie made a mental
note of Sofya's role.

"Who did I become?" Adam asked.

"I'll wait to reveal that bit of information."

What an active night everyone had. Perhaps Adam is no longer trustworthy!
Ellie looked around the circle and noticed that Angel and Jack, her
previous students, hadn't said anything. "Who are you guys?"

"I couldn't sleep all night. I kept hearing all those sounds of wolves,
and I just kept waking up. But I know I haven't changed. I'm still the
same person I was last night." Angel was new to the village, and Ellie
wondered if she could trust her.

Jack laughed, "I was drinking all night, and I think I may have
forgotten who I am now. I don't think I did anything bad though. In
fact, most likely, I am innocent."

"Well, we're going to have to eliminate someone, and since you were drinking, there's a chance you could have done something bad without realizing it." Mikael pointed an accusing finger at Jack.

"That's a possibility, but I wouldn't bet on it."

"Carina, you've also been pretty quiet. Who are you?" Ellie asked.

"Oh, I'm quiet because I'm just a normal villager, so I actually don't have any information," Carina replied, as she glanced around the circle, seeming to challenge anyone to call her a liar.

Carina was Ellie's oldest friend in the group, and she felt like she had a pretty good understanding of her friend's character, so she was inclined to believe her. Ellie added the new information to the chart:

Role	Task	Who???
Seer	Can see one other character	Ellie!
Hunter	If voted out, can choose one other person. If he chooses a bad person, the good team wins, if he chooses a good person, the bad team wins	Adam??
Troublemaker	Trades the cards of two other characters	Sofya
Insomniac	Can see their card at the end of the game	Angel
Robber	Takes another player's card and becomes that character	
Drunk	Trades his card with one card in the middle, but doesn't look at it	Jack
Villager (2)	No special task—normal good person	Mikael? And Carina
Werewolf (2)	Bad character! If he is killed, the good people win	Mikael???

| Minion | Bad character! If he is killed, the bad team wins |
| Tanner | Bad character (but on his own team)! If he is killed, only he wins |

The group of friends kept talking, trying to figure out who could possibly be a werewolf, who was innocent, and who was suicidal. The safety of the village depended on finding and killing the werewolves, but there were a couple of characters who would not help the good team win if they were eliminated. Everyone had to analyze the situation and judge carefully between good and evil.

"Does anyone have any floss?" Angel interrupted the conversation to ask the group.

Ellie was about to answer when Mikael jumped in.

"Why do you need floss? Are you trying to escape suspicion by leaving the village meeting?"

"No, I just have a piece of meat stuck in my teeth from dinner, and I wanted to try to get it out. Besides, I already gave all of my information, and I don't think there's anything else I can say to help."

"What kind of meat were you eating last night?" Mikael continued the interrogation while Ellie pointed to some toothpicks nearby.

"I already told you, I couldn't sleep. I was just eating some beef jerky."

" Right . . ." Mikael glanced at Sofya. *Don't believe her,* he mouthed. Hey, you never told us what trouble you made last night. What did you do to Adam?"

"Yeah, who is he now?" Ellie asked. Since Ellie knew Adam had been good, she wasn't inclined to put him on trial even though several people seemed to think Mikael's theory about her and Adam being werewolf partners seemed legitimate. They had suggested putting Adam on trial, but Ellie also wanted to wait to see who his new identity was. His trial really depended on that.

"I switched him with Jack." Sofya glanced from Jack to Adam. "So, Jack the drunk is now doubly suspicious."

If Jack really is the drunk, and Sofya is also telling the truth, then that means no one is the hunter. But who could the werewolf be?

Mikael turned to Ellie again, "Who did you say you are?"

"I told you! I saw that Adam is the hunter. And he confirmed it."

"Of course he would confirm it if you are both bad together."

"Come on. You have to believe me. I don't know if we can trust Adam now—depending on if Sofya is telling the truth, and who Jack was, but originally, Adam really was the hunter."

"Ok, Adam, right now, you are just the normal village drunk." Mikael turned his attention to Adam. "So, if you and Ellie were bad before, you can tell us now."

"I really was the hunter!" Adam continued to insist.

"As long as Adam keeps backing up Ellie's story, we can trust them, but if he backs out of the story, we definitely have to put Ellie on trial. If Jack is telling the truth, then the hunter is in the middle now. But Jack is still possibly suspicious because he was the drunk even though Adam has the drunk card now." Mikael addressed the village. He was again controlling the entire village. If he was evil, then they had to be careful of him, but Ellie really did think he was innocent today.

The discussion continued as the sun rose in the village, and everyone ate more gummy bears and Orion cream pies. Accusations went back and forth. Should they kill Jack as a possible suspect, or Angel, because her alibi was so weak? What about Ellie if Adam turned on her? Everyone argued, fighting for their innocence, and trying to sway the votes in the way they wanted.

"Mikael, who are you going to eliminate?" Ellie finally asked.

"You." Mikael smiled.

"If you want to lose, then fine, eliminate me, but that's the worst choice you could possibly make!"

"Hmm, that's not such a great defense, but I'm just kidding. I don't

hink it's actually you. Ok, it's time to vote, people. Remember, you
get one chance, and you can't change your vote. You also must vote
when I finish counting down. No delays or your vote won't count."

Ellie held her breath. This was the moment of decision. She had
o choose, but she still wasn't sure. Anthony was really quiet, but that
vas normal. In fact, he had barely spoken except to say that he didn't
eally understand the rules. Maybe it was him, but for some reason,
Ellie suspected Angel. She didn't like agreeing with Mikael, but she
vas pretty sure he would vote for her, and this time she was sure he
vas right. She ran through the chart in her mind one more time:

Role	Task	Who???
Seer	Can see one other character	Ellie!
Hunter	If voted out, can choose one other person. If he chooses a bad person, the good team wins, if he chooses a good person, the bad team wins	No one
Troublemaker	Trades the cards of two other characters	Sofya
Insomniac	Can see their card at the end of the game	Angel???
Robber	Takes another player's card and becomes that character	
Drunk	Trades his card with one card in the middle, but doesn't look at it	Adam
Villager (2)	No special task—normal good person	Mikael and Carina
Werewolf (2)	Bad character! If he is killed, the good people win	Angel??? Mikael?

| Minion | Bad character! If he is killed, the bad team wins |
| Tanner | Bad character (but on his own team)! If he is killed, only he wins |

"3...2...1...vote!" Mikael's voice rang through the village.

A moment later, the votes were calculated. Several people had voted for Ellie and Jack, but the most votes pointed toward Angel. Ellie held her breath as they all followed Mikael into her house.

"Yes! We were right!" The house was full of the broken plates and claw marks from Angel's nighttime alter-ego. The clues to her fellow werewolves were also revealed, and they were immediately executed. The villagers had succeeded in foiling the plans of the werewolves and other bad characters.

The group of friends stood up and stretched. They had been playing werewolf, a Mafia-style game, for the last three hours, and it was getting late.

"Anyone feel like a movie?" Mikael grabbed a handful of M&M's and wolfed them down. It's a holiday, and the night is still young!

"Speak for yourself! It's already after midnight!" Ellie was glad the girls had a room upstairs in the loft apartment they had rented for the short holiday. "Hanging out is super fun, but I'm still exhausted! You all watch a movie if you want!"

Changing Times (Diary of a Young Wife)

Becky, Anne, Samantha

Inspiration Words: Strawberry and Sweater

December 3rd

I haven't had time to write in my diary for so long, but Samantha just texted me, and it reminded me of university, when I used to write in my diary more often. So much has happened, and I can hardly remember those days when my biggest struggle was what to eat for dinner or if I would ever be able to understand my foreign teachers.

I haven't seen Anne and Samantha since my wedding a couple months ago, so I'm super excited that Samantha invited my husband and me to her house for a Christmas party next week! During university, I often celebrated Christmas with them, and I'm really looking forward to doing it again.

I actually almost forgot about Christmas because work is so busy right now, since it's the end of the year. I'm teaching elementary school students, and I love it so much, but it's so much work to plan lessons and make sure all the students are listening and then take pictures and send all the pictures to their parents after class. My husband, Alex (Samantha suggested that as an English name when Alex asked her for a recommendation in choosing an English name), says I spend more time sending messages to parents than I do actually teaching lessons. I think he's exaggerating a little bit, but sending all those pictures does take a lot of time. I guess it makes the parents feel more involved in their child's education.

Anyway, my big decision right now is what I'm going to wear. Every year, we get a different Christmas item to celebrate with together. Our first year, we all got Christmas mugs. Mine was painted red with gold buttons to look like Santa's coat. It even had two handles on the side that were designed to look like his arms. The second year, we all had Christmas hats. I got reindeer antlers, but Samantha's fluffy Santa hat was everyone's favorite. We all took turns taking selfies with that one.

This year we are going to do Christmas sweaters! I can't wait to choose my sweater! I already started looking on *Taobao* (tow bow— rhymes with how, a Chinese version of Amazon), and I found a couple I really like. But I can't decide if I want to get the silly sweater with a reindeer or the pretty sweater with a nice snowflake. I'll probably get one I can wear to work also, but there are some really funny ones that I love! There's a red one with a green 3D Christmas tree that looks so cute and fun. There are also a few reindeer ones that would look great with my reindeer antlers if I can find them. When Alex and I moved to our new house, I might have thrown them away.

I love our new house, but it's so expensive. I had no idea that buying a house would cost so much money. We had to get one that's a little farther from the city because the ones in the downtown area are ridiculously expensive! I don't know how anyone can afford those. Alex's parents gave us a little bit of money, but it was nowhere near enough to be able to afford a house close to where we work. So, we just have a nice long subway ride every morning. Thankfully, we can ride most of the way together.

I'm a little worried though about what will happen when we have kids. I really want to have kids before too long, but Alex keeps saying we need to wait. He always reminds me that kids are expensive, and we don't have much extra cash right now. And when we do have kids, what are we going to do about school? Most of the good schools are in the city center, which means we might not be able to send our kids to the best school. But we didn't have a choice, since we could only afford a house on the outskirts of the city. Maybe we can move back to Alex's hometown, which is a smaller city. The houses will be a little more affordable, and the schools will probably be closer. But now that we've lived in the city for several years, it will be hard to go back to a small town. The big cities are just so interesting and convenient.

Another problem with going back to Alex's hometown is that then we will be really close to his parents. They're both very nice, but I don't know that I want to live with them or close to them. They will probably move in once we have kids, and I guess it will be nice to have someone to help take care of the kids, but I don't know. I like having time alone with just Alex and me. Wow. So many things to think about lately! Maybe I can talk about some of these things with Anne and Samantha—they always seem to have good ideas, even if they don't completely understand the Chinese system.

~Becky

December 12th

I haven't had a chance to write about the party yet because the weekend was so busy and I've had a lot to do at work. The party was so much fun, and I'm so glad Anne and Samantha planned it for us. We all had really cool sweaters. Alex and I decided to get matching ones with little reindeer on them and alternating red and white stripes.

Anne and Samantha both had cute sweaters too. Samantha had a Christmas tree one, and Anne got a snowflake. Her boyfriend, Johnson, had a Santa Claus sweater. Our pictures all look so cute, and I'm glad we did a Christmas sweater theme!

We also made Christmas cookies together! Alex and Johnson had never been to one of our parties, so it was fun to teach them how to decorate the cookies. Samantha had already baked them, so we just frosted the cookies. It took a really long time, though, because we kept stopping to talk. We all had so many things to talk about! It was the first time I met Anne's boyfriend, and I'm so glad she has a Chinese boyfriend. I'm hoping that means she will stay in China forever! Samantha doesn't have a boyfriend yet, but I think she will also marry a Chinese guy.

After we frosted the cookies, Samantha brought out a big surprise! She had made chocolate covered strawberries! Actually, I think Anne was the most excited about it. I thought they were tasty, but they were a little too sweet.

Anne and Samantha both wanted to hear all about our new house, so we showed them lots of pictures and asked them to come and visit is sometime. I really hope they can, but it's a little far away, so I'm not sure if they will be able to soon.

Even though I was so tired after the party, I'm so glad I got to see my friends. While Alex and Johnson were talking, I went into the kitchen with Anne and Samantha and I told them all about my thoughts about having kids while we washed dishes. They were really kind to listen, and I already feel better just after talking about it. And they also reminded me that I don't have to think about it too much yet because even after I have kids, they don't have to go to school right away. "There's still time!" Samantha kept saying.

And they're right. I wish everything were clear now, but since it's not, I can just enjoy this part of life now. And who knows what will happen next. Maybe the next time I have a chance to write in my diary, I will have a kid!

~Becky

Just a Flower
Lili

Inspiration Words: New and Flutter

Lili (lee-lee) sat in the dirt. She picked up a discarded can and began filling it with dirt, pretending it was tea for her and her imaginary friends. A moment later, she dumped it back into her hands and tried to form a ball. It was too dry, so she went over to the garden where her grandma was watering the vegetables and pulling weeds. She scooped up a little water and managed to take enough back to make a damp ball of mud, which she then kneaded like dough. She had seen her grandma doing this to make steamed buns.

As she worked with the ball, Lili's short black hair fell around her face. In primary school, she and most of her friends had a similar hairstyle—short, cut just at their jaw lines.

The sun warmed her skin as giant clouds floated overhead. Lili was glad it was summer. After a long winter of snow and cold, the bare trees had slowly showed the beginnings of new leaves, and flowers bloomed. Now the heat of summer had arrived, but Lili was happy to be home from school and outside with her grandma. She wondered if maybe her mom would even come back to visit them sometime.

"Time to go inside, Lili," her grandma was standing right behind her, but Lili had been so consumed with her mud dinner preparations and wondering when her mom would come next that she hadn't even noticed.

"Ok," Lili stood to walk inside with her grandma. At the steps, Lili ran up to the potted flowers that she had helped her grandma to plant earlier in the spring. She had watched eagerly for the first bloom, but every day, the green plants were still just green. Today, however, as she ran up to the plants, she noticed a bit of color in the Impatiens plant's pot (feng xian hua, fung xee-en hwah). At first, she thought it was just the flutter of a butterfly's wings, but as she got closer, she noticed that the butterfly was hovering over a tiny blossom.

"Grandma, the flowers are ready!!! Come over here and see!" Lili hurried back to pull her grandma over to the flowers. "Look! This one is pink!"

"Sure enough! I'm going to go inside and start making dinner. Why don't you pick the flower petals off and put them in a bowl and bring them inside?"

"Ok!" Lili hurried back to get the can she had been playing with earlier and began pulling the flower petals off the plant and putting them into the can. She could hardly wait to see the beautiful colors dye her fingernails. When they planted the flowers, her grandma had promised to use the flower petals to make a dye to color her fingernails once the flowers bloomed. She had been waiting for so long, and she was so happy that it was finally time!

When she had collected all of the pink petals she could find, Lili ran inside. Her grandma was bent over the stove, a large pan smoking from the hot oil and peppers that filled the air with one of Lili's favorite aromas.

"They're ready, Grandma! I got a lot!"

"All right, put them in a bowl and mash them. You can use that one over there," Grandma motioned to a mortar and pestle that she had just used to smash the garlic. "Make sure to wash it first or your fingernails are going to smell like garlic!"

Lili rinsed the remaining fragments of garlic out and dumped in her flower petals. She began mashing them while the pot let out another hiss as grandma added some vegetables.

After a few minutes, Lili ran back to her grandma. "Is this good enough?"

"Hmm, keep mashing them up. We want there to be lots of color or it won't make much difference to your nails. But first, here, let me add some alum." Grandma reached into the cupboard and sprinkled some white powder on top of the flower petals.

"What's alum?"

"It's a chemical that will help the color to stay on your fingernails longer."

After dinner, Lili helped her grandma wash the dishes. She dried her hands on the front of her shorts and picked up the pot of smashed flower petals. Grandma got a small cloth and helped Lili put the petals in the cloth. Then, she wrapped the cloth around each of Lili's fingernails, with the petals against her fingernails. Next, she tied it with some string so the cloth would stay in place. Finally, she ripped up a plastic bag and tied a piece of plastic around the cloth on each finger.

A few minutes later, Lili started to pull the plastic and cloth away from her fingers.

"Not yet; it's not ready yet." Grandma pressed the cloth back down.

"But can I look just a little bit? I want to make sure it's working!"

"If you look too early, then it won't work."

"Ok." Lili pressed the cloth against her fingernails. "Grandma?" Lili asked.

"Yes?"

"Do you think Mom will like my beautiful fingernails?"

"Of course she will." Grandma brushed Lili's hair back from her face.

Grandma stood up, took out some dough and started to make some *mantou* (mahn-toh, steamed bread) for breakfast the next morning. Lili had noticed that her grandma didn't like to sit down—she was almost always doing something, usually cooking.

After she had finished with the dough, Grandma told Lili to go get ready for bed. "When you wake up in the morning, your fingernails will be a beautiful pink! You will also feel cool and fresh—you know this kind of nail dye is really good for our health."

The next morning, Lili woke up and brushed her hand against her face and was surprised to find the plastic covering still on them. She almost forgot about her dyed nails! A second later, she was ripping the plastic and the cloth off to look at her fingernails. They were perfect! She stared at her nails, admiring the pale shade of pink.

Lili ran downstairs to show her grandma who was already up and fixing breakfast for Grandpa.

"It worked, Grandma!" Lili cried, running up to her grandma with her fingernails displayed in front of her.

"Looks nice," Grandma said as she stirred porridge on the stove.

"Grandpa, look!" Lili bounced across the kitchen to her grandpa next.

"That's very nice," he smiled at her and put his hand on her hair.

"Can I go play with Nana (nah nah) and show her my nails? Maybe I will even let her have some of the flowers so she can do it too! I wish Mom were here so I could show her too!"

Tuning in and Tuning out

Yao Bo

Inspiration Words: Yellow and Jealousy

Yao Bo (yow bwoh) sat in his spoken English class, but his mind was far away. His mind often escaped to quieter places during this class. When his university teacher told them to ask each other a list of questions to practice their English, the room quickly became loud. Yao Bo didn't have a partner, and he didn't try to find one. Sometimes he would think about the questions, but usually, he would allow his mind to wander to a quieter place.

The brown wooden desk was smooth under his fingers, and Yao Bo's eyes drifted to the window. The classroom was on the fifth floor, and he had a nice view of the blue sky past the beige curtains. He saw a bird and allowed his gaze to follow the bird for several minutes.

"Hi, Mike!" Yao Bo turned at the sound of his English name to see his foreign teacher standing next to him. "What genre of music do you like?"

"What is 'genre'?" Yao Bo tried to imitate the sound of the difficult word.

"A moment ago, I explained that *genre* is a type of music." Yao Bo's teacher smiled patiently and glanced around at the other students who were still talking among themselves.

"Oh, I don't know."

"Do you like pop music? Or jazz? Or hip-hop?"

"Maybe pop." Yao Bo wished his teacher would talk to someone else. The class was so noisy, and he could feel his heart rate increasing.

"Do you have a favorite singer?"

No such luck. Yao Bo thought about any names of English singers he knew.

"You can talk about a Chinese or a Western singer."

"Umm, maybe Jay Chou (choh)?"

"Oh, nice! That's great! Which song of his do you like?"

Yao Bo looked down at his desk. As he did so, he remembered an older desk from his days in middle school. That desk had a yellow surface with metal legs. He had shared it with another boy, but they didn't talk much. Yao Bo never knew what to say to him, and the other boy didn't really seem to care about being friends.

Compared to college, middle school seemed easier. Yao Bo enjoyed most of the classes because everyone was quiet and knew where to go and what to do. Out of all of the classes, history was his favorite. In history class, he didn't have to speak much. Instead, he just listened to the teacher and read the passages. During one class, his teacher turned on a song. Jay Chou started singing about his eternal love for someone. He sang about the Babylonian king and the Mesopotamian plain and his immemorial love. All of the students were quiet as they listened, and Yao Bo found himself feeling the beat of the music. The drums kept the time, and a guitar added a bit of melody behind Jay's voice.

Yao Bo returned to the present and looked at his thin, American teacher who was still standing next to him, but was also motioning to two other students to continue talking. He cleared his throat, and his teacher looked back at him. "I like a song called *Ai Zai Xi Yuan Qian* (ah-ee dzie ssee yoo-ahn chee-ahn). I don't know the English name."

"That's great! What's the song about?"

"Hmm, I haven't listened to it for a long time." He pulled out his phone and tried to find the song, but he was nervous, and he kept opening the wrong apps before he finally managed to find the music app.

"Ok, you can find it, and I'll be back in a minute to hear about it." His teacher walked away, and Yao Bo breathed a sigh of relief.

He found the song and glanced through the lyrics. He did enjoy listening to Jay Chou's songs, but he had no idea why he had mentioned this song. It wasn't one of the ones he usually listened to.

A few minutes later, his teacher returned. "The English name is, Love before B. C.'"

His teacher looked at him, puzzled. "Can you explain that a little more?"

Yao Bo glanced back at the lyrics. "That's the translation of the title, and it's about a man who has imm . . .em . . .orial love for someone. There's a lot about history in the song too."

"That sounds like a really interesting song! Thanks for sharing it

with me. Do you think you could find a classmate to talk with also?"

Yao Bo glanced around the room. Everyone was paired up in nice groups of twos or threes. Some kids might have felt jealous of the closeness that many of his classmates had with each other, but he was content to sit to one side at the front of the room, distant from everyone.

"It's ok. I'm fine by myself." Yao Bo looked down at his book and tried to pretend that he was going to be working hard studying the vocabulary words in front of him.

"Ok, well make sure you're prepared to answer the questions in case I ask you."

Yao Bo nodded and looked back towards the blue sky outside, the beat of the song still keeping time in his head, drowning out the noise around him.

It's Going to Get Better, Right?

Lena and Andrew

Inspiration Words: Trash and Twist

"How do you describe 'the worst day in the world' in English?" Lena asked her Australian husband as she shut the door to their home, took off her shoes, and collapsed onto the sofa.

"Umm… Horrible? Awful?" Andrew, her husband looked up from the book he was reading.

"No. Worse." Even though Lena had only started using English with the other foreigners when she came to China from Russia seven years ago, she could already communicate easily. She already knew these words, and she knew they weren't strong enough.

Andrew paused, trying to think of a suitable word. "An astronomically bad day? A catastrophically bad day?"

"Astro— what? Whatever it means, that sounds more like it."

"Ahh, I've got it! A terrible, horrible, no good, very bad day." Andrew declared triumphantly and then laughed.

"Sure. But it's not funny."

"Of course not, sorry for laughing. It's just a quote from a children's book my mom would read me when I was young. What happened?" Andrew asked, moving closer to his wife.

"Well, this morning when I got to class, they told me the class was canceled. But I didn't have time to come home because I had my other class not long after that. So, I woke up early for nothing and I had to just sit around wasting time. Then the students in the next class were dead. Like, they refused to answer any of my questions and several of them even fell asleep. They fell asleep! In class!"

"Oh, that's super frustrating."

"Yeah, the next class was a little better, but most of my classes were just horrible today. I couldn't figure out why the students were so tired until one of them said they had to wake up super early for some kind of flag-raising ceremony before their normal morning classes started—I think that's why the first one was canceled. It was such a long day."

"That does sound miserable. How about we eat some dinner? I'm sure you'll feel better after eating." Andrew glanced over to the table. "Wait a second, I thought you were going to pick up some dinner on your way home?"

Lena dropped her head against the back of the sofa. "I was. I bought it and hung it on the handlebars on my bike. I should have asked him to double-bag it, but I thought it would be okay. It wasn't. On my way home, I hit a bump when I was coming off the edge of the sidewalk. Somehow the bag split open, and everything fell out. Everyone was driving past me and staring at me while I tried to pick it up and salvage some of the food, but it was hopeless, so I just threw it all away."

Andrew put his arm around Lena's shoulders and pulled her close to him. "It's okay. I'll order some delivery right now. It should be here before too long."

"It gets worse. Just now, when I was in the elevator, I checked my phone and saw that our landlord sent me a message. I translated it, and I think she said we have to move. I don't want to move again!" Lena took out her phone and was tempted to throw it across the room. But instead, she handed it to Andrew, whose Chinese was much better.

Can you read it and tell me if our landlord really is kicking us out?"

Andrew took the phone and bent his head over it, studying the characters on the screen carefully. After several moments, he put the phone down. "Yes, she said she is remodeling her other apartment, and they want to live here while they're doing the remodeling."

"NO!" Lena cried in frustration.

"But she did say we have until August to find a new place and leave."

Lena checked the calendar. "That's four months away, but our contract ends next month. What if she changes her mind next month and says we have to leave earlier?"

"Maybe we can start looking for a place, but we don't have to get it too quickly unless we find one we really love?"

"Hmm." Lena didn't want to look for a new apartment, and after such a horrible day, she didn't even want to think. Mainly she just wanted to sit on this sofa and wish that the world would just stop and give her a few moments of peace.

No such luck.

She looked around at the rug and the set of shelves in the corner. They had just finished getting this apartment set up, and it finally felt like home. She had only moved in a couple of months ago after they got married, and she wasn't ready to move again.

"Let's pray that God will give us a really good apartment in this neighborhood." Andrew said. "And let me order some food so we can eat dinner."

The next week, Lena opened the apartment-hunting apps she still had on her phone. She hadn't deleted them from last year when she and Andrew had found this apartment, with the goal of living here for a long time and hopefully starting their family here.

Lena clicked through various apartments, wandering through the virtual rooms that were shown on the app. Once she found some she liked, she would contact the agents, but she wanted to know what was available first.

After Lena found several that seemed promising, she talked to the agents in the area and asked to see the available apartments in the same neighborhood. She and Andrew both loved the location and had no desire to go further away from the subway or further away from Lena's job. She already had to ride her bike for thirty minutes, and she didn't really want to have to wake up any earlier.

Every evening for at least a week, they visited different apartments. The first few were pretty terrible. Even though Lena insisted that she only wanted to look at ones she had found on the app, the agents invariably took them to some awful places first to lower their expectations.

After looking at several places one evening, Lena and Andrew sat down back in their own home to talk over what they had seen.

"They're all terrible!" Lena complained. "That last one smelled awful, like it was full of dog poo. And the one before that looked like it was being used as an extremely overcrowded office. The bedroom didn't even have any beds, and there were desks all over the living room and in all the rooms."

"Yeah, these ones definitely weren't ideal, but it's gonna be all right. We still have time to find a place that will work for us."

Lena was already scrolling through her phone, trying to find another one that maybe the agents hadn't showed them. "I just can't believe that those nasty apartments are the only ones available in our price range. Our range isn't even very low!"

"Maybe we just need to give it some more time. But even if that last apartment were clean, I didn't like how much traffic you can hear from the road."

"Me too. And I also hated that they had the dumpsters right next to the entrance of the building. Smelling an entire building's worth of trash is not how I'd like to start my commute each morning."

The next night, they visited another apartment, and the moment they walked in, Lena knew they had found their home. "This is it!" She and Andrew walked through the living room, bedrooms, and bathrooms, their smiles getting bigger with every step. This one even had two bathrooms!

"How much is it? How long can we rent for? When can we move in?" Lena and Andrew ran through the normal list of questions with their agent, and everything seemed perfect. The price was about the same as their old one, and they could rent for two years instead of just one.

While they sat on the bed in the master bedroom, Lena grabbed Andrew's hand. "I think we should make an offer now. We don't want it to disappear while we're trying to decide, and this one seems really perfect. The living room is nice and big, there are two bathrooms and several rooms so we can have guests over. I don't think we can find one better than this."

Andrew didn't respond for a moment as he ran through his mental list and tried to imagine them living in this apartment. "It does seem pretty good. Let's walk through once more just to double-check everything."

Lena bounced through the apartment while Andrew followed slowly behind, making sure the cupboards opened easily and nothing was broken.

"Ok, let's do it." He finally said to Lena.

They finalized the decision with the agent and made a plan to meet with the landlord to sign the contract. They were relieved to find a place so quickly, and Lena was already thinking about where to put everything in the new apartment.

The next day, Lena threw her phone on the couch, trying to suppress a scream of frustration.

"What's wrong?" Andrew asked.

"The landlord won't rent to foreigners."

Forced back to where they had started, Lena pulled out her phone and started looking for another place. "Next time we need to remind the agent to tell the landlord we are foreigners, and make sure it's ok before we look at the house and fall in love with it."

After several weeks and many more houses in the same neighborhood and nearby, Lena and Andrew started to feel the pressure of finding a place. They looked at apartments with super high ceilings and super low ceilings, old places with broken floor tiles, and newer places with a child's graffiti splayed across the living room wall.

Finally, they walked into an apartment that was much emptier than most. A small couch sat in the corner with a wooden coffee table in front of it, and the rest of the living room was empty. Large light fixtures that looked like a twisted collection of metal hung from the ceiling in the living room. The walls needed some paint, but it was clean and large.

"I actually kind of like this one." Lena glanced around the living room. "I mean, the lights are definitely gonna have to go, and we might need to paint it, but . . . what do you think?"

"It's nice. We could put our extra chairs along that wall, and this will be a nice little area to entertain guests."

"And the landlord allows foreigners, right?" Lena asked Andrew.

"Yep. The agent made sure of it," Andrew put his arm around Lena's waist and smiled. "So, do we have a deal? Did we find our new place?"

Lena looked around the sparse room, the stark white walls turning a warm ivory in her imagination as she pictured new lights overhead. She heard their laughter as they played boardgames with friends, and she could smell Andrew's coffee brewing in the morning as they watched the sunrise through the wide window.

"We found our new home," Lena answered, beaming up at him.

The Airplane's Ghost

Xueqing

Inspiration Words: Smoke and Flag

Wang Xueqing (wahng ssee-yoo-eh cheeng) stared at the words in the Hamlet play. They were supposed to read the first act for homework, and she was really trying. But as she was reading, she had to look up every three words in the dictionary on her phone, and she feared she would never get through it.

"Kun Na (koon nah), do you understand what's going on in this story?" Xueqing leaned her chair back to talk to her friend who was bent over the same book moving her lips as she read silently. "I've read a summary in Chinese and the first three scenes, and all I know is that there are a lot of names, and someone important was murdered."

"Yeah, this is a really hard one." Kun Na looked up from the book on her desk. "The king was murdered, and now he's appearing as a ghost to his son, who is Hamlet. I think the ghost wants Hamlet to get revenge on the guy who killed him."

"Ugh . . . I know I should care, but this is just so hard to read."

"I know, it's hard for me too."

"And your English is amazing. If it's hard for you, I feel like I should just give up now."

"Come on, I'll help you. Maybe it will get easier later, like our teacher said."

"I wish we didn't have to study British literature. It just seems impossible. It seems like everything we read is so hard to understand."

"Yeah, I'm really worried about the midterm exam."

"Me too . . ." Xueqing dropped her head onto the book.

The next day in class, Xueqing tried to listen as her teacher talked about the play, but she kept using English to talk about it, and Xueqing couldn't force her brain to focus after more than a few minutes. Two of the boys slipped out the back of the classroom to "use the bathroom" but everyone knew they were going out for a smoke.

Xueqing hated smoking, and she hated that the boys skipped class to do it, but she was also wishing she had a reason to leave.

A plane flew past out the window, and Xueqing followed the flight with her eyes. A long, white trail traced the path where the airplane had flown, and she wished she could paint the scene. She imagined a shining plane in the middle of a bright blue sky, and a string of white lines dotting across the canvas. As the trail began to disappear, she decided she would call her painting "The Airplane's Ghost."

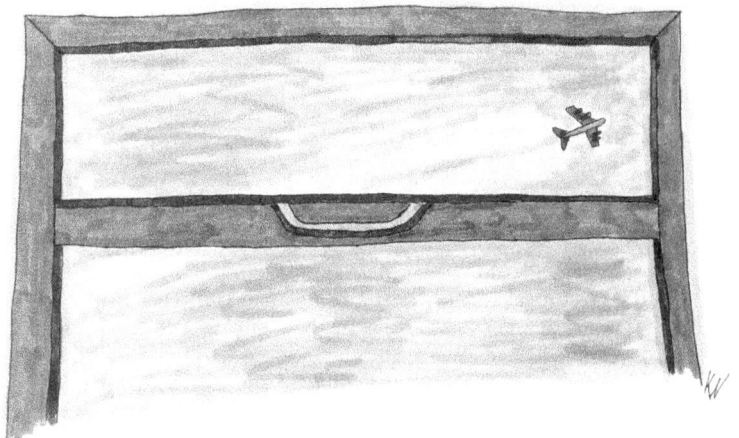

"Xueqing, what do you think?"

At the sound of her name, and even worse, her name at the beginning of a question, Xueqing looked at her teacher.

"About the ghost?" Xueqing asked, hoping she was guessing right.

"I just asked the class what you all think about Hamlet's plan to act crazy so he can discover the truth."

"Oh, that's why he was acting crazy," Xueqing muttered to herself while her classmates giggled. She knew they were mostly just relieved they hadn't been called on, and she rolled her eyes at her own bad luck. "I think it's a pretty good plan." *Please don't ask why*.

"What makes it a good plan?"

Xueqing groaned and glanced at Kun Na for help. Kun Na pointed her notebook in her direction, but Xueqing couldn't decipher the words.

Finally, she looked back at the teacher. "Well, I can't think of any other ideas to find out why his dad was murdered, so it seems like a good plan to me."

The teacher responded and moved on to another student, and Xueqing stared back at the impossible words in front of her.

She knew she should try to pay attention, but her eyes drifted back to the blue sky outside. The airplane's trail was almost invisible by now. As much as she hated studying British literature, Xueqing knew she hadn't enjoyed Chinese literature much more. Maybe that's why she was here now. Perhaps if she had paid more attention and tried to understand those stories back in high school, she would be someplace else now. Her mom's voice echoed in her brain again: *Studying for one more minute means that your husband will be different.*

The boys came in from their smoke break and sat down in their seats on the back row. They hadn't even opened their textbooks. *I think I should have studied for another minute. Or maybe several thousand more minutes.* But as Xueqing thought back to those days, she knew she couldn't have done anything differently. And even now she wasn't making much of a difference because she still couldn't manage to force herself to study half as much as she should.

Maybe I won't get married. And to drive any prospective guy away, I'll pretend I'm crazy. Xueqing smiled and focused her gaze on the window again, fixing the palm trees, the tops of the white buildings, and the brightly colored flags in front of the library in her brain so she could include them in her painting.

Penultimate Memories

Anne and Johnson

Inspiration Words: Penultimate and Precious

"Today is our penultimate day in Hunan (hoo-nahn) with your family."
Anne and Johnson sat together on the couch in Johnson's parents'
living room. Johnson's dad was at work, and his mom was out buying
vegetables for dinner. His sister and her husband had also disappeared
for the afternoon, and Anne was enjoying some quiet time in the
normally-noisy apartment.

"Hmm," Johnson replied.

Anne knew he hadn't understood *penultimate*, but he was too comfortable on the couch to ask what she meant. She switched into
Chinese and tried again. "This is almost our last day here before we
go back home."

Johnson murmured an incoherent reply, and Anne gave up trying
to draw him into conversation for now. She leaned her head back
against the pillows on the couch and stretched her feet over the wooden
box with the electric heater inside. They shared a blanket and even
though Anne could see her breath, as long as she kept her feet and
hands inside the blanket, she was pretty warm. Most of the houses
she had visited over the last few weeks had similar styles of heaters,

although a few were starting to use central heating systems. But she liked this box because it kept her feet nice and toasty.

The room was dim, even though it was mid-afternoon. Once again, it was raining. During their stay with Johnson's family, they had only seen the sun for a grand total of three days out of three weeks.

Anne sat staring at water dripping off the corners of buildings for several more minutes. Suddenly she stood up and slipped half-way into her house shoes that were next to the couch. Johnson didn't open his eyes, and Anne nudged him firmly. "Come on, you can rest tomorrow night on the train. Let's do something fun!"

"But this is fun!" Johnson insisted, pulling the blanket up to his chin.

"Well, we've been sitting here for an hour, and it's time to do something else that's fun." She pulled the blanket off of him and started hunting around for some house shoes that he could wear. She usually knew where hers were—unless they got pushed under the couch or a table, but Johnson somehow always managed to lose his.

"We're going for a walk!"

Johnson groaned in response, and Anne pulled the blanket off of him again and began pushing him toward the edge of the couch. He managed to drag himself off the couch, and several minutes later, they were out the door and walking down the street.

Johnson held a pink umbrella over them that Anne had grabbed on their way out. For several minutes, they walked quietly, and Anne thought about the many things she had experienced in the past several weeks with Johnson's family.

She couldn't think about the trip without remembering New Year's Eve with Johnson's family, his sister, and his brother-in-law's family. The food had been delicious, even though there were lots of things she hadn't been able to identify.

Anne eyed the meat dishes suspiciously. Every time she tried to get some meat out of a tasty-looking dish of duck or lamb, she would come away with intestines or bones. So, she avoided them, and let Johnson fish out the pieces of meat that he knew she would enjoy.

Sometime during the middle of the meal, hongbao *(hohng bow, red envelopes filled with money) were passed out from the older generation to the younger generation. Anne hardly felt young enough to receive anything along with the children, but they insisted that since she wasn't married, she must take the offered* hongbao. *Anne hesitated, unsure whether she should keep refusing or just take it. She glanced at Johnson, but he was reaching for some food. Finally, she accepted the red envelope, hoping she wasn't breaking a social code for doing so.*

After the meal, everyone moved to the couches. They casually chatted while absently watching the Spring Festival Gala, an hours-long TV program consisting of various performances interspersed with upbeat announcements from the hosts and hostesses. While the younger members of the family were on their phones Anne was trying to decipher the meanings of the skits.

A moment later, Johnson's sister jumped up and cleared off the coffee table in the center of the room.

"We're going to play a game!" She announced.

Anne loved games and eagerly watched to see what kind of game this would be.

Johnson's sister placed various bills in a line down the center of the table. She smoothed them flat before picking up a can of coke.

After completing these arrangements, Johnson's sister looked at the watching family members. "For the reasonable price of fifty yuan, you can try to roll this can down the table. If the can stops on a bill, you can keep that money."

"That's way too expensive!" Johnson protested as he looked at the chances to win mostly fives or tens with only a couple of fifties or hundreds thrown into the mix.

"No, it's not! Come on! Try it!"

"Definitely not, make it cheaper, and we will." They argued for several minutes until Johnson finally asked for a trial round.

"You can't do a trial, but I'll let your girlfriend try it once for free," his sister finally compromised.

Anne stood at one end of the table and rolled the Coke can gentle down the line. It came to a stop on top of a ten-yuan note. Johnson cheered for her, but Anne was already ready to try again. She found the hongbao she had received during dinner and pulled out a hundred. "Do you have change?" She asked.

"Come on, just play twice, then I don't have to give you change!"

Anne laughed. "Ok, fine. You got me." Anne prepared to roll the can once more, keeping her eye fixed on the hundred in the center of the table. The can began rolling and slowed as it reached the hundred-yuan note. "Stop! Stop! Stop!" Anne shouted at the can.

"Go! Go! Go!" Johnson's sister shouted at the can. The can kept rolling just past the hundred and stopped on a twenty as Anne groaned. During her next turn, she *came away with nothing. The can had stopped between the fifty and the hundred notes.*

The family took turns rolling the can down the line of money; the singing and dancing on the TV forgotten as they shouted at the can to stop or keep rolling.

Anne smiled at the memory. "What was your favorite part of our trip?" She looked over at Johnson.

He thought for a moment; then looked back at her. "I like showing you different places from my childhood while we walk around."

"Like this school?" Anne pointed toward the empty building that Johnson had told her was where he went to elementary school.

"Yep."

"And that time you got robbed under the bridge?"

"Well, that's not the happiest memory, but I'm glad I could tell you about it."

Anne squeezed his arm. "I'm glad the guy didn't hurt you."

"The people who robbed us were just bigger kids. Even though they had a knife, I don't think they would have done anything. They just wanted to scare us."

"Still, I don't like it." Anne shivered.

"It was a long time ago."

Anne and Johnson walked in silence for several minutes. "My favorite memory is the Eve of Spring Festival. I loved that game your sister had—even though I ended up losing eighty yuan."

"Yeah, that was fun."

"Your family is pretty precious, and even though I can't wait to go home and get my own food and wash my own dishes and my own clothes and not be so cold all the time, I will miss your family."

"You miss washing dishes?"

"I miss the freedom to do things for myself instead of always feeling like I'm intruding if I try to help."

"Ahh, yeah, they are always like that since I don't come home very often. I like it."

"I like it too. I'm just looking forward to having my own space again."

"Yeah, me too."

Anne and Johnson continued walking down the street with the rain dripping gently down on the umbrella above them.

It's been a good trip, Anne thought.

Goodbye
Braxton

Inspiration Words: Breath and Dragon

Braxton closed the door and turned the key in the lock. For the last time. He had already finished clearing the memorabilia off of the walls and cleaning everything with his staff. He had thanked them all, wished them well, and said goodbye. That was yesterday. Today, he wanted to say goodbye one more time. To the place. He had believed in this restaurant, and he had fought for this restaurant when he probably should have given up long ago. He had worked long hours when he couldn't afford to hire more staff, and he had advertised tirelessly. And now, it was all over.

He looked through the glass windows to the bare walls. It was almost worse coming back now when everything and everyone were gone. He could still remember all of the high-energy nights when the tables were filled with customers. Hearing the silence and Seeing empty tables with chairs turned upside-down on top of the tables just made him feel sad.

He and his wife had bought plane tickets to return to the States, and they were scheduled to leave next week. Just a few more days to get their whole lives packed up or given away. He was exhausted from trying to find people who would buy or take the things they had collected over the years.

But today, Braxton had told his wife he would be gone for most of the afternoon and evening, and she understood. He needed a walk-about. She had coined the term many years ago. At first, she had been worried and frustrated when Braxton would disappear for hours at a time. When he returned, she would demand to know where he had gone. *"Oh, just around the city."*

"What do you mean 'around the city'?" She had replied, letting out a frustrated breath. "I've been waiting to have dinner with you for two hours! It's 9 p.m.! I was so worried that you had been in an accident!"

"But I told you I would be home late today."

"If you finish work at 3:00, then 'late' is 5:00."

Braxton had apologized, and over the years, Braxton had learned to be a little more specific about his plans. His wife had also learned that he needed time to wander, taking in the city and absorbing the energy around him.

Today was one of those days. He needed time to think, and he needed time to not think. Rather than taking the subway to a new location and exploring that area, Braxton decided to walk around the places he had come to know and love.

The side streets near the restaurant were small, and lots of shops and restaurants crowded together under the apartment buildings. Little boutiques with an assortment of clothes, along with small cafes and all sorts of restaurants, drifted past his steps. As he walked, Braxton thought about the years he had spent walking these streets.

Suddenly, hundreds of loud explosions jerked his gaze to the other side of the street. A dragon dance began outside of a restaurant with a huge archway. Large bouquets of flowers lined a red carpet that led to the entrance. A new restaurant. Braxton paused to watch the dragons bob around on top of sticks held by dancing performers. The move-ments simulated a dragon swimming through the air, ducking its head and slithering its body up and down and back and forth. *These guys are pretty good. The restaurant must be expecting to do well if they can afford this kind of performance on opening day*. Braxton couldn't help but think about the irony of seeing a new place open on the day he closed his own restaurant.

They must be so excited. And terrified. Braxton remember his own excitement, but he also remembered that fear. He remembered worrying that they wouldn't survive the first year. But they had. They had survived many years, and it had taken a global pandemic to finally close his doors. There was no shame in that.

A couple of performers in lion costumes joined the show, and a crowd of people had stopped to watch, cell phones capturing the acrobatics as the two people inside each lion performed incredible jumps and dances. While they jumped around, each person managed to keep in sync with the person inside the other half of the lion to create the semblance of a real creature. The dragons were red, but the lions were mostly yellow. First, the lions pranced around on the ground before moving on to more complicated stunts using a couple of tables.

More firecrackers continued to attract the attention of those passing by, but Braxton soon decided to move on. He had seen plenty of dragon dances, and although this one was good, he wanted to continue his walk-about.

Braxton turned toward Canton tower and the river. When he came toward the end of the small shops, he had to go into the tunnel under the road. Once across the road, he found the park where people often went jogging in the evening. A few walkers enjoyed the shade from the trees, but most of the joggers were probably still at work.

The small creek running through the center of the park was pretty dry, but several sprinklers kept the grass and flowers healthy. The sun was getting lower by the time he arrived in Hua Cheng Square (hwah chuhng; flower city square). Canton tower rose up into the blue sky in front of him. The library and the museum stood to the left of the square, and the opera house with its long ramps and unusual lesign stood on the right. Other buildings bordered the square, but he square itself was clean and empty. A few people flew kites, and 3raxton looked up to see a kite in the shape of a black bird.

The square didn't have many people, and Braxton walked right lown the center of the square with Canton tower directly in front of aim. Before he could get to the river, he turned right to walk through he giant outdoor stadium. He had once seen a concert here, but now he seats were empty and only a few people walked across the stage)ecause that was the fastest way to reach the river.

A grassy area next to the river reminded him of afternoon picnics vhen his kids were younger, and they would sit in the grass and enjoy he breeze in the brief Guangzhou (gwahng-joh) autumn. When he urrived at the bridge, he crossed the river. By the time he reached the)ther side the sun was disappearing and the lights under the trees were urning on. The lights on Canton tower were also more visible now, und Braxton smiled as he gazed at the tower that was now a rainbow)f lights and a moment later, blue; then purple; then orange. Always :hanging. Just like the city.

Braxton followed the tree-lined path next to the river until he was tired of walking. The joggers had come out, and the darkness was complete. Groups of older women danced together with synchronized movements to the beat of music projecting from large speakers. He would hear the music a few minutes before seeing the group and, as he passed, the music would disappear as well. A couple of the groups contained men and women who danced together in a ballroom style dance with a more melodic musical accompaniment, but the majority of the groups used the strong, upbeat music with a loud bass—square dancing (so named because it was usually performed in a large open square).

Canton tower was no longer in sight, and after he passed another crowd of women arranged in neat rows waving their arms and moving forward and back in time with the music, Braxton realized he was ready to go home. Maybe he was also ready to go back to America, but a part of his heart would always be in this city, the place where his dreams had come true and died.

Time to make new dreams.

ACKNOWLEDGEMENTS

I'm one of those people who almost always reads the acknowledgements section of a book. I like seeing behind the scenes and into the author's life and world because it helps me understand a little more about how the book I just read came to happen. The book you are holding in your hands would have been impossible without the help of many people. This is my first time to self-publish a book (don't get any ideas that I've published regularly—nope, this is my first book ever and a dream come true). But in order for you to hold this book in your hands, many things happened first.

Megan Hutchinson is the Lewis to my Tolkein (This is wishful thinking, but hey, we can dream, right? Maybe my next book will be an epic.). She is the reason my fun writing exercise turned into a book. I asked her a little over a year ago if she would send me a couple of words so I could write my Word Doodle, and after I wrote a handful of them, she encouraged me to keep going and turn them into a book. Knowing that I am not usually a proactive person, she also sent me a video about how to do it and kept encouraging me to follow this path.

So, in addition to sending me words every week or so, she also was the first to read all of the stories and smile about people that she recognized in the pages. Later, when I started the editing stage, Megan labored over every story with me, refining the conflicts and characters and making sure that everything would be clear to someone who has not been in China for extended periods of time. She is an editor that any writer would love to work with (and she did all that in addition to teaching a crazy class schedule—literally crazy).

Kendra Ness is my incredible illustrator. I couldn't have asked for someone I would rather work with for the illustrations. Seeing my stories come to life in the form of art was so exciting. I love the flavor that her art adds to the stories. Her style is cute and fun, and I realized that is exactly what I wanted for this book. Kendra sacrificed her own time and energy to make sure that these pictures were done when I needed them (especially when I kept changing my mind about what I wanted), and I'm so thankful for her work to make my crazy dreams a reality.

Peter Reid is a professional designer, and when I realized that I didn't want to spend lots of frustrating hours staring at a computer that didn't do what I wanted it to do, I went to Pete (some self-publishers do their own typesetting, but that sounds like a nightmare to me!). I was thrilled to find someone who knows how to make computers cooperate and was willing to help with the design of my website and the beautiful book that you are holding in your hands. Pete has his own UX Design company here in China, and I feel so lucky that he was willing to take care of all the design for the website and book.

I would often visit Pete and his wife, Dasha, throughout the process, and Pete would always patiently show me what he was working on and how things were going. He used Kendra's artwork to design the website and the book cover, and I loved seeing the process unfold. I remember when Pete said that he had a prototype for the book cover ready. Before I saw the cover, I was so nervous. Since Pete was a good friend, I wasn't sure how to tell him if I didn't like it, but when he finally revealed the cover, it was better than anything I could have imagined. I'm thankful to have had such a talented designer working on this project with me! And thank you to Dasha, Pete's wife, for your support through this entire process as well.

Thanks to Miranda Regan for sharing the concept of Word Doodles with me during my first year in China. I have a lot of incredible memories from that year, but some of my favorites are sitting around Miranda's apartment and listening to her latest Word Doodle. I really hope that she turns her Word Doodles into a book someday, and if she does, you should definitely buy it, because her stories are brilliant.

I'm also thankful for all of the people who read the stories and offered advice. I wanted to get input from Chinese friends to make sure that I represented their culture and their people accurately and positively. I'm going to use their English names (if they have one) because that's easier for me to type and for my American audience to read. Thank you, Jaye, for your enthusiastic response to reading the entire book and offering detailed comments about things that you noticed. Thank you, Kaye (my Chinese English teacher friend), for your brilliant advice about so many things and for catching so many errors! Thank you, Shirley, Brandon, Jiamei, Ruby, and John for reading the stories and giving feedback.

I also need to thank all of my other readers. Thanks Albert Wolfe (your thoughts about having repeat characters and having characters from different stories meet and interact was so much fun!), Tyler Hill, Ruthie Burrell, Jessica Wu, and Mom and Dad (aka Ruth and Dennis Mullins) for your comments. You have all been to China for varying lengths of time, and your insight into everything was incredibly helpful. Thanks so much for your excellent comments.

These stories would be impossible without the people behind the stories. I would never be able to list the names of all of the students and friends who have made these stories possible. I'm so thankful to the students that have allowed me to be a part of their lives. I'm thankful for the students who opened up to me enough to share their stories and their struggles. Thank you for welcoming me into your lives and your cultures. Being here in China has completely changed me, and I hope that reading these stories has changed you a little bit too. I have met some incredible people over here, and I'm honored to be able to share some of those people with you.

I want to thank Mom and Dad. Many parents wouldn't have allowed their daughter to travel to the other side of the world, but my parents have trusted God with their fears and loved me and supported me throughout my journey in China. I'm honored to be the daughter of such great people!

And thank you to you, my dear reader, for picking up this book and reading it (even the acknowledgements!). I pray that you understand a little more about this great world that we live in and some more of the incredible people that God made. God bless you!

ABOUT THE AUTHOR

Alison Mullins has lived in China for nine years teaching in universities, teaching middle school, and studying Chinese. She first fell in love with writing in elementary school and has been planning to publish a book ever since then (*Amanda and the Missing Kitten* being the most primitive attempt). She loves reading, writing, hanging out with friends, and having adventures.

ABOUT THE ILLUSTRATOR

Kendra Ness has been studying Mandarin Chinese for more than thirteen years. She and Alison became friends while taking language courses in Guangzhou, China and have remained close ever since. As a hobby, Kendra has been drawing for the annual Inktober challenge every October since 2014. This is her first attempt at illustration. She also hosts a podcast called "The PatchworkGirl and Friends" where she talks about life, music, movies, TV shows and everything. She provides a cover illustration for each episode as well.

KNOW MORE

Visit my website (www.alisonmullins.com) and let me know about your favorite characters. Also check out the website for words if you want to write your own Word Doodles.

RESOURCES APPENDIX

If you are interested in teaching in China and would like more information about teaching or guidance, visit **atlasteaching.com**. The game that Becky talks about is hands down my favorite game to play on the first day of class. This blog explains in detail how to play that game and also gives ideas for other games and tips for teaching.

Teach like a Champion **by Doug Lemov** also has some useful tips for teaching.

Fluentu.com is another great website for ESL tips.

If you are interested in learning more about the cultural differences between America and China, *The Culture Map* **by Erin Meyers** helped me a ton in understanding the different cultures.

Powerful, Different, Equal **by Peter B. Walker** is another interesting look at the cultural, historical, and economic backgrounds of China and America and how those differences affect us today.

On China **by Henry Kissinger** is another resource that talks about the history of China. After reading this book, I feel like I understand some of the more sensitive aspects of Chinese history.